OUR LOVE REPLAY

A NOVELLA

SHIRLEY SIATON

OUR LOVE REPLAY
A Novella

ISBN 978-1-961052-76-5 (paperback, romance)
ISBN 978-1-961052-80-2 (paperback, discreet)

1st Edition, May 2024

Published by Shirley S. Parabia
Cover design by Temptation Creations
Interior formatting by Champagne Book Design

Inky Sword Book Publishing
Barangay Quezon, Arevalo, Iloilo City 5000
Republic of the Philippines
inkysword.com

Content Warnings

Warnings for content of an explicit nature.

Recommended for mature readers 18 years old and above.

PLAYLIST

'Everywhere'
Michelle Branch

'I'm With You'
Avril Lavigne

'Far Away'
Nickelback

'Private Emotion'
Ricky Martin & Meja

'No Promises'
Shayne Ward

'Walk Away'
Solid HarmoniE

'214'
Rivermaya

To those who loved and lost

And to the ones who are found

CONTENTS

ACKNOWLEDGMENTS

I am very grateful to MOD Filipina Magazine for giving my short story, 'Leaving the Mountain,' the inspiration for this work, the opportunity to be read the world over.

Many thanks to Rein Geronimo for the line art pieces featured at the beginning and end of this novella.

OUR LOVE REPLAY

A NOVELLA

PROLOGUE
THE RAIN

Tara

I N AN ODD DANCE OF BLACK AND GREY SWIRLS, THICK clouds gathered overhead, promising a downpour that would soon drench the pathways of the university.

Sighing, Tara Galvez tore her gaze away from the sky and turned her attention to the retreating back of her best friend. She raised a hand in farewell just before the other girl disappeared around a corner, in a quick getaway before the heavy rains hit.

Jasmine's parting words lingered at the back of her mind, both a comfort and a challenge. *"You really should share those poems with other people, just like your grandmother says. They're too beautiful to stay hidden in that tiny notebook of yours."*

Alone now, she felt the familiar wall of shyness close around her. She hugged her canvas bag closer to her body, feeling the first whispers of wind nudge her along, urging her toward the library before it closed for the day.

Moments later, with the reserved History book snugly

under her arm, Tara headed towards the closest campus gate, hoping the traffic wouldn't be as bad as Jasmine had feared. As she made her way down the library steps, she nearly collided with a lanky boy in a red varsity jacket. He was an upperclassman, all limbs and hasty apologies as he darted past, his backpack swinging haphazardly from one shoulder. She blinked in surprise, watching as he disappeared towards the grounds in the opposite direction. It was then that she noticed a large rectangular notebook lying on the concrete.

"Excuse me! You dropped something!" she called out, but he was already too far away to hear her.

Sighing, she bent down to retrieve the fallen item. As soon as she touched the dark blue linen cover and thick spiral-bound cream paper inside, she realized it was a sketchbook. Curiously, she flipped through the pages, each one filled with pencil strokes so vivid they seemed to pulse with life. Flowers rendered with delicate lines bloomed around majestic mountains; bodies of water rippled and rows of coconut trees swayed across pages; and faces captured in silent conversation stared back at her.

Debating whether or not to follow the young man, she glanced towards the direction he'd disappeared, then up at the sky. Dark clouds loomed closer, reminding her of her own need to get home. The best thing to do would be to get to the jeepney stop immediately. She could hand over the sketchbook to the college office in the morning. Not that it was something expensive or anything…

Or was it?

Before she could think twice about it, Tara found herself scurrying in the same direction as the upperclassman, the sketchbook clutched tightly to her chest. The distant echo of bouncing basketballs drew her onward, until she caught sight of the open-air court at the end of the grassy field.

Of course. With his varsity jacket, he could very well be part of the team. She'd heard about the city-wide intercollegiate basketball tournament opening game next week. Everyone in her class had seemed very excited about this, talking about another championship.

The sidelines were packed with people, many of whom were girls, all eagerly watching the team practice despite the imminent rain. She squeezed through the throng, murmuring apologies right and left. As soon as she had a clear view of the concrete court, she spotted the sketchbook's owner almost immediately. He was clad in jersey number one, tearing down the court in a blurry zigzag while dribbling a basketball with his left hand.

Tara looked around her tentatively before turning to address an older girl standing next to her. "Excuse me, do you know who the boy wearing number one is?"

The girl responded with an openly curious stare. "Why do you ask?"

She swallowed, feeling her cheeks grow warm under scrutiny. "Um, I need to return something that belongs to him."

"Seriously? You don't know who he is?" The girl shook her head disbelievingly. "That's Lucas Delgado. He's a junior and the star player of our varsity team. He pretty much single-handedly made us win the city-wide tournament for the past two years. Everyone here wants him, and everyone else out there, too. He's that hot."

Both girls watched as Lucas moved across the court, skillfully evading his teammates and effortlessly sinking a three-pointer. Tara felt an unexpected flutter in her chest as she took in his lean build and the way his wavy black hair stuck to his forehead from sweat. It was easy to see why he was so popular.

"Call out to him," the girl urged. "If you got something for Lucas, he won't mind. He's nice, too, you know. We have a few classes together."

Tara felt heat rushing up her neck at the mere thought of talking to jersey number one. "Uh, no, it's okay. I think I'll just wait until the end of practice."

"Suit yourself." The older girl shrugged and turned back to watching the players, eagerly chatting with other people around them about the team kicking the butt of the maritime academy down the road from their college.

Tara retreated to the shelter of a nearby acacia tree, careful to keep Lucas in her line of vision. As the minutes passed, her mind wandered to the beautiful sketches she had glimpsed, wondering how someone so talented on the basketball court could also have such a gift for art. It seemed almost unfair, and, yes, undeniably intriguing.

Just then, Lucas made an impressive layup shot that sent the crowd into a frenzy of cheers and applause. She couldn't help but join in, her heart racing as she watched him turn away from the ring and look in her direction, a smile on his face. The fleeting contact made her realize he had deep-set, distinctly piercing dark eyes; he also had a dimple in his right cheek. But, as quickly as Lucas had glanced her way, he ran off again, this time to guard his opponent at the other end of the court.

The first droplets of rain splattered against the ground, darkening the earth and turning the sky an ominous shade of gray. The drizzle quickly escalated into a full-scale downpour, sending spectators running for shelter.

To her surprise, her feet remained rooted to her spot, her eyes never leaving Lucas as the practice game continued without missing a beat. Lightning streaked across the sky, followed by a loud thunderclap.

"Practice is over!" the coach finally yelled. "Everyone, head inside!"

Determined not to lose sight of jersey number one, Tara fixed her eyes on his tall form as he gathered his belongings and jogged off the court with his teammates towards the main college building. She couldn't let this opportunity pass her by; she had to return his sketchbook.

"Lucas!" she called out, but her voice was drowned out by the rain and the rumble of thunder overhead. Resolved, she followed him, her sandals squelching as she made her way gingerly around puddles.

As she stepped around a tree, its branches and leaves swaying in the wind, Tara's foot slipped on the muddy path.

She cried out in surprise as she toppled onto her backside, her things falling from her grasp. Strangely, the sketchbook remained glued to her grip, as if unwilling to be let go.

"Are you okay?" Lucas Delgado stood over her, rain dripping from his hair and basketball jersey. He had her canvas bag and borrowed History book clutched in his hands.

She blinked up at him, taking in the look of concern written across his face. It took a few seconds for embarrassment to sink in, a few more for shock to follow.

"Y-yes, I'm fine," she stammered, her throat tightening as she attempted to push herself upright. Pain shot up through her left ankle, causing her legs to wobble beneath her.

"Here, let me help you." He extended his hand, and she gratefully took it. As she rose, he noticed his sketchbook in her other hand, his eyes widening in recognition. "Is that my mine?"

"Sorry," she mumbled, her face burning despite the coldness of the falling rain. "I saw you drop it earlier, and I wanted to return it to you."

"Don't be," he replied, shaking his head. "Thank you. And I think these are yours." He handed over her bag and library book with a small smile.

Then, without warning, he scooped her up into his arms, eliciting a surprised gasp. Ignoring her, he went on conversationally, as if he did this with people on a regular basis. "You shouldn't be walking on this slippery path. There's an open classroom nearby where we can wait the rain out."

Lucas carefully made his way out of the field and onto

the wet pavement, his hold on her as steady as his heartbeat beneath her ear. As the rain continued to pour around them in a thick veil of water and wind, it felt like they were the only two people in the world.

"Hang on, okay?" He was looking down at her with a gentle smile. It felt strange to hear him say it, considering he was the one doing the heavy lifting. "We're almost there."

She nodded, ducking her head behind her bag so he wouldn't see how flustered she really was. It took a few more long, rain-drenched moments before he stopped in front of a partially open doorway that led to an old classroom next to the cafeteria.

"I have Biology class here," she said lamely, acutely aware of the heat and closeness of his body.

"Good enough, then." He used his shoulder to push the door open, stepping inside the dimly-lit room. He made his way straight to the teacher's table up front and carefully lowered her onto the wooden surface.

"Are you okay?" he repeated, this time examining her more closely, his dark eyes searching hers.

"Y-yes," she managed to say through her dry throat, struggling to retain a semblance of composure. "Thank you."

"You're welcome." He made his way back towards the entrance and attempted to switch on the lights. He cursed softly when nothing happened.

"I think the power's gone out," she offered.

"Yeah. Good thing I'm with you and not my teammates."

The comment made her blush, but she chose not to

clarify what he meant by it. Instead, she tried a safer topic. "My best friend's gone home. I hope she doesn't get stuck in traffic. She lives in Jaro, so it's a two-ride commute."

"I live in Jaro, too. How cool is that? I'm trying not to think about how long it will take me to get home." He grinned sheepishly and pulled up a chair by her feet, sitting down and placing his backpack next to her on the table. "What's your name?"

She decided she liked having him close, even though all she ever did was redden and stutter at his proximity. He had a solid, reassuring presence. She got the same feeling looking at his drawings earlier. No wonder she'd followed him to the court. "Tara Galvez."

"Nice to meet you, Tara. I'm Lucas Delgado." He offered a friendly grin that melted away most of her nerves. "You were at the court earlier, weren't you? I saw you by the acacia."

"Um, yes. I picked this up at the library after you dropped it. You were in a hurry so I don't think you heard me calling out." She handed his sketchbook over, careful not to let her hand touch his. "I followed you to return it."

"Thank you. That's very kind of you." His eyes and face lit up as he flipped through the pages. "This is my favorite one. It has drawings of my father's childhood village in Antique province. I try to add more every time I visit, which is not very often these days."

Moved by the wistful tone in his voice, she imagined him roaming through the rural landscapes, capturing the beauty of life in pencil and pastel. She could see it now...

Lucas seated on top of a grassy hill, sketching intently with a furrowed brow; herself next to him, writing poetry in her own notebook as a gentle breeze ruffled her hair.

"Let me take a look at your foot," Lucas said suddenly, jolting her back to reality. He put the sketchbook in his bag, the look of concern back on his face. "May I? It's the left one, isn't it?"

Blushing even more furiously, she nodded her assent, her eyes carefully trained at a spot on the wall above his head as she shook her wet sandal off.

With sure hands, he lifted her compromised foot and examined the ankle with gentle presses and light twists. "It doesn't seem too bad. Good news is that it's not even sprained. You should be fine after resting it for a bit. I'll stay with you."

"Thanks." She tried to quell her embarrassment at the easy familiarity and openness he treated her with. She could hardly believe that this kind, attentive young man was the same star athlete who took over the basketball court and captured the attention of so many girls.

"Are you a freshman? I don't think I've seen you around before today." He gave her ankle a reassuring pat before moving backward to a more respectful distance. The girl on the court earlier was right; he really was nice.

"Yeah, I just started this semester." She tried to muster a smile, hoping it made her look less awkward than how she really felt.

"Welcome to the college, then," he replied warmly, his

eyes crinkling at the corners as he smiled in return. "I hope you're enjoying it so far."

"Thank you. I am." *Especially now*, she wanted to add, but couldn't find the guts to say so, not in a million years.

"Great! You should come see our games. Next week we'll be mopping the floor with those maritime snobs next door. Just because we're part of a state university doesn't mean we're all scrawny nerds, right?"

She nodded vigorously, unable to look away from the animated expression on his face. "I heard the girls talking about it earlier. No, we're definitely not all scrawny nerds, that's for sure."

Lucas leaned back in his chair, seemingly satisfied at her response. This time, his gaze zeroed in on her curiously. "So, Tara, tell me about yourself. What do you like to do in your free time?"

She hesitated before giving him a truthful answer, hoping she didn't sound like a 'scrawny nerd.' "I, um, I like to write poetry and sing."

"Really? That's awesome. You must be really talented. Are you joining the theatre group, then?"

"No," she mumbled. "I can't do all that dancing I've seen them do. Besides, these are just hobbies, nothing more."

He shook his head. "Still, I'd love to hear you sing someday, maybe even read some of your poems."

Before she could respond, he noticed her shivering from the cold air seeping through the windows. "Hey, you're getting soaked. Here, take my jacket."

"You don't have—" she protested weakly, but was interrupted when he took the garment off and draped it over her shoulders. The warmth from his body radiated from the shiny fabric, instantly enveloping her.

"You know, your hair's really beautiful," he murmured, adjusting the jacket by gently flipping her hair over it. "Like you."

Her breath caught in her throat, her heart pounding so hard she thought it might burst from her chest. She didn't know how to react to his compliment, so she simply stared at him, admiring the dimple on his cheek as he looked at her with a soft, almost dreamy, smile.

"Better?" His eyes lingered on her face for a moment longer before turning to the drenched campus outside. "You should be warmer now."

"Thanks," she muttered, her cheeks burning with a mix of embarrassment and gratitude.

They sat in companionable silence for a little while longer, watching as the rain began to subside. When the downpour eventually turned into a light drizzle and the fluorescent lights overhead flickered back on, Lucas stood up and stretched his long limbs.

"Looks like the worst is over." He turned back to look at her as he slung his backpack over his shoulders. "We should get going. Get a move on before it pours like hell again. You're okay getting home, aren't you?"

Disappointment, unbidden and unstoppable, crept into

her, causing tightness in her throat. "Yeah. I live in Molo, so it's just one ride from the highway."

"I'll walk you to your stop, then." He held out a hand, the gesture so casual it was hard to believe they didn't know each other two hours ago.

Trying her best to ignore the storm of unfamiliar sensations within her, she took it, feeling the strength in his grip as he helped her to her feet. She slid on her damp sandals, grateful for the absence of pain from her ankle, as she watched him shake off rain water from her bag and the History book.

"Thanks." She held out her hands for her belongings, but he shook his head.

"I got it," he said, in a tone that begged no argument. "You're okay to walk? Do you think you can use my jacket as your umbrella? It will keep you dry for the most part."

With her things safely in his hands, he led the way out of the classroom. The college lay quiet and serene in the aftermath of the downpour. They walked along the rain-slicked, glistening path illuminated by the yellow-orange glow of campus lamps, their footfalls echoing against the empty buildings.

They crossed the highway carefully to Tara's jeepney stop, Lucas moving to either side of her against the oncoming traffic. Once they reached the waiting shed, half of its cement seats dampened by rain, he gestured for her to sit on a relatively dry corner. "Here's hoping you can get a ride soon."

She shivered slightly, feeling the cool air on her damp

skin. She reached to remove his jacket from her shoulders, with every intention of returning it.

"Keep it," he insisted, shaking his head. "I'll feel better knowing it got you home safe and warm."

"Thanks," she murmured, sliding her arms into the garment's expansive sleeves. It was several sizes too big for her, but the heft of the extra fabric felt almost like an embrace.

Silence descended on them as he sat down next to her. She gazed out into the drizzling night, watching droplets of rain reflect the lights of the highway and the vehicles passing by, listening to the hum of engines and the patter of water on concrete.

She glanced at Lucas and, strangely, his eyes met hers squarely. He gave her an effortlessly reassuring smile; his gaze seemed to hold a thousand secrets, alluring and mysterious. An unfamiliar warmth spread through her chest and down to her stomach, an involuntary response of her body that both terrified and thrilled her.

Finally, a Molo jeepney appeared and he stood up to flag it down, the vehicle stopping before them with a screech of its brakes. He handed over her things, his fingers brushing against hers for a fleeting moment.

She found herself wishing she could hold on a little longer to his touch, maybe even stay in the cover of the rain; hidden by water, wind and shadows, suspended in time.

"Good night, Tara," he said softly. "I'm sure I'll see you around. Thanks again for giving my sketchbook back."

"Bye, Lucas." With one last look into his eyes, she

climbed aboard the jeepney, settling onto the only vacant seat at the edge.

As the vehicle pulled away, she watched him wave, remnants of his smile still on his face, his tall figure growing smaller as the distance between them increased.

She didn't look away until he was out of sight. She leaned back against the seat, feeling the steady thrum of the engine beneath her as the rain-soaked city rolled by outside.

She clutched her bag and History book tightly to her chest, both still bearing traces of the warmth of his hands. She closed her eyes, as if to calm the whirlwind of emotion and confusion within her, all caused by their chance encounter.

Although she couldn't see anything, her heart seemed to know something for certain—whatever it is she had just shared with Lucas Delgado, this was only the beginning.

It was three A.M.
I began to cry
Remembering what I left unsaid

Remembering how I last saw
You as you walked away
It was three P.M.

~ Excerpt from 'Time's Three'
Lyrics and music by Tara Galvez
I Remember You, Esta Melodia Records

CHAPTER 1

THE ARTIST

Tara

A GENTLE BREEZE RUSTLED THROUGH THE TREES, carrying with it the sweet scent of fresh blooms. Tara walked along the winding path of Galvez Farms, savoring the feeling of her hair dancing around her face as she hummed softly to herself.

As she passed a cluster of coconut trees sheltering a patch of earth she'd chosen as her personal garden, her fingers instinctively traced the delicate petals of the gold and white flowers she had planted weeks back. The vibrant colors seemed to sing to her, bringing a sense of peace and inspiration. This was her sanctuary, the place where she had hoped to find her music…and, perhaps, herself.

She paused in her walk and leaned against a tree, the strains of a new melody on her lips. She let her eyes flutter close, as she thought of the chords she needed to write down the minute she got back to the villa. Just then, her phone buzzed in her pocket, momentarily breaking her creative trance.

Tara pulled out her phone to see Jasmine's name flashing on the screen. She could feel a smile tugging at her lips, a momentary reprieve from the pressures of composing the next big Spotify hit. "Hey, gorgeous."

"Hello, yourself. How's Asia's Acoustic Angel doing so far away from the studio? Spread your wings yet—or did being too far away from city life clip them?" The voice of Jasmine Samontes carried through the line as if she were right there on the farm path, eagle-eyed and equally sharp-tongued.

"If I do decide never to leave the farm, it's all your fault. You won't believe it, Jas. I've just finished another song for the album. It's all coming together so beautifully here."

"Really? That's amazing!" If there was one constant thing about her manager, it was the ability of knowing exactly what Tara needed, even before she realized the same herself. "I told you this would be the perfect place to find your inspiration. Where it all began and all that…and how's everything else going, girl?"

"You should see the flowers I've planted, Jas. They're absolutely stunning."

"Ah, I can only imagine," Jasmine sighed wistfully. "I miss those days when I still had time to visit the farm. Send me pictures, though. And when you're ready to rejoin the old ball-and-chain, please come back with some of your magic *biko*, will you?"

She laughed at the request; her grandmother's secret recipe of the traditional sticky rice cake was legendary—and Tara knew how to make it perfectly. "Of course. Least I could do after you put everything on the line for me."

"This is about you, Tara." The response was uttered gently, but there was steel behind it. "It's about making sure that magic in you gets the chance to shine. Not all of us have something as special. I'm just glad I was able to convince the studio you needed this time off. Besides, there won't be a 'line' without your music. So, yeah."

She swallowed at the sincerity and determination in Jasmine's voice, feeling guilt churning in the pit of her stomach. "Thanks, Jas. I needed this." *More than you'll ever know.*

"Honestly, you don't have to thank me. I'm just doing my job."

"Still, it's the best idea we've had in all these years. I thought without my grandparents this place would feel different. It does feel different…but it's like they're still with me, somehow, telling me to let the world hear my voice."

"Trust me, I can feel it," Jasmine replied enthusiastically.

"Just remember, don't rush the process. I know that's just not gonna cut it for you. The songs will come when they're ready, and when they do, they'll be all the more beautiful for it."

Tara could feel hot tears trying to fight their way out from behind her eyelids. Yes, she needed the time, but the real reason wasn't as simple as her best friend thought it was.

It was a reason that had haunted her since her second album, *I Remember You*, reached platinum a few years ago. It was a reason that had haunted her since the studio began planning an international concert tour to celebrate her tenth year as a recording artist, to coincide with the global release of her much-anticipated third album.

"I hope you're right," she said, praying Jasmine couldn't hear the tremble in her voice. "I hope I don't let you down. And everyone else, for that matter."

"You won't, songbird," came Jasmine's firm response. "Now, just focus on making some more of your beautiful music. I can't wait to hear it all."

"As you say, boss. By the way, how's everyone? Your parents? Jared?"

"Mama and Papa are keeping busy as usual. You know how they are, academia is life. And Jared's out of the picture. Life's too interesting for me to be tied down to a nerdy sound engineer who plays *Fortnite* in his spare time." Jasmine's tone was dismissive and no-nonsense.

"You okay?"

"Why wouldn't I be? I'm having fun right now keeping the media at bay. They pretty much think you're off on a much-needed vacation before your big tenth anniversary celebration, preferably somewhere exotic. Beaches, white sand, margaritas, all that. They don't know you're working on your biggest album yet. And they definitely don't know you're in Antique."

Tara giggled. "Let's keep it that way for the rest of the year."

"I'll do my best, songbird, and then some. Listen, enjoy your time there. When you're ready to return to us, we'll be waiting."

The words landed with the finality of a staunch businesswoman who knew the rhythms of the music industry as well as her own heartbeat. Tara could only wish she had her best friend's command of the world around them, as well as Jasmine's unshakeable belief in her and her talent.

After they exchanged goodbyes, she slid her phone back into her pocket and resumed her walk towards the farm's main villa, her eyes lingering on the white walls perched like a pearl amidst the emerald sea of coconut leaves.

The sun was already high in the sky, lavishing warmth on her skin as she, as always, made her way alone. Soon, as was now her routine, she would sit down on the dining table for lunch, a solitary meal in the company of her thoughts and memories.

Her thirties had arrived quietly, more poignant than

she would ever dare to admit. Her fourth decade in the world was heralded by the loss of both her paternal grandparents. Even with an impressive lineup of hit songs and countless sold-out appearances, within her grew a sense of isolation and uncertainty. Not even Jasmine's constant encouraging presence and the adoration of her fans could alleviate the heaviness in her heart.

In an attempt to distract herself, Tara pulled out her phone and checked her meticulously curated social media accounts, tagged in numerous discussions with varying speculations on her current whereabouts. Her last public appearance had been in the New Year's Eve countdown show of a popular TV network. Some claimed she had eloped with an unidentified non-showbiz boyfriend, while others insisted she was ensconced in some far-off resort, most likely overseas, penning songs inspired by the sea.

If only it were that simple and straightforward. With a sigh, she replaced the phone in her pocket, a sad smile forming on her face even as her eyes took in the almost dream-like coordinated swaying of fronds in the breeze.

Creating music about love was a far cry from the romantic life people believed she lived. In truth, her career had always been a demanding companion, leaving little room for anything else. Her only true confidantes had been her guitar and her worn leather-bound notebook. Even Jasmine and her parents—her lifelines to reality—remained shielded from the depths of her innermost fears.

As she stepped through the wooden sliding doors

that led to the villa's spacious living room, her gaze fell on a framed cut-out from her college paper's literary section, proudly displayed in its place of honor on her grandparents' wall. The cut-out, flanked by childhood pictures of Tara and her brothers, featured her first published poem, 'The Voyage,' accompanied by a delicate drawing of a boat sketched by none other than Lucas Delgado.

Lucas.

The kind, talented boy who saw something special in her poetry. He'd drawn every single illustration for the paper to match her poems for two years before he left school and started his glittering basketball career. Her grandmother had all those other poems with Lucas' illustrations compiled in an album, tucked away on the shelves of the villa's library.

Tara recalled the shy, quiet girl she used to be, hiding behind her guitar and notebook, pouring her heart out into her music and poetry. And there was Lucas, who had carried her to safety and warmth that fateful rainy evening her freshman year. She had wanted to talk to him again after that night, but never had the chance.

Her fingers traced the lines of the drawing, each stroke evoking admiration for the boy whose smile remained a sweet but heartrending memory, always filling her with longing for what could have been.

If only.

If only things had been different. If only she had said something to him after that night.

"I hope you've found happiness," she murmured to the framed poem, aware of how ridiculous she'd look and sound to anyone else watching.

Tara's thoughts turned inevitably to Lucas Delgado of the present, now a household name in Philippine basketball. The staff of Galvez Farms and their families—hell, the entire village and town itself—rooted for Lucas and his team. Whenever his team had a game, everyone asked to go home early to watch it.

She had followed his career closely since he'd graduated, cheering him on from afar. Outside of the hardcourt, he was the star endorser of the liquor brand that owned his current basketball team; he also represented a casual clothing line and an international cologne brand. She had seen his pictures at those glamorous galas and parties, beautiful actresses and models draped over his arm, and had wondered how he was doing in his personal life. She knew he was successful—a franchise player, touted to lead his team for a third Philippine Cup championship in the coming months—but what about his heart?

Was he the same gentle soul she met back then, who didn't hesitate to help a girl he didn't even know? Did he have someone who saw him not only as a sports superstar but a gifted artist, whose illustrations told stories a million times better than words ever could?

A tear slid down her cheek as she brought her fingers to her lips and pressed a kiss to Lucas' signature. Her heart swelled with a mix of admiration and pride for this man she now barely knew, but whose presence always lingered in the delicate, most guarded depths of her memory.

"Good luck, Lucas," she whispered. "I wish you all the best. Always."

She forced herself to turn away, telling herself this would be the last time she'd cry over someone who had most likely forgotten about her a long time ago.

But she knew her heart, as always, refused to listen.

CHAPTER 2

THE PLAYLIST

Lucas

THIS WAS THE KIND OF PLACE ONE CAME HOME TO. Lucas Delgado could not blame his parents one bit for their choice of retirement home, as far as it was from the town proper. As he drove the rented SUV towards the sprawling bungalow he'd only seen in pictures before, he could feel a sense of relief, a lightness he couldn't last recall ever experiencing in the big cities.

"Hey man, you made it there yet?" The voice of Derek Torreblanca, his closest friend and teammate for six years now, rang through the car speakers as they conversed over the phone.

"Yeah, almost at the new house," Lucas replied, his eyes taking in the groves of coconuts that lined the wide dirt path. "It feels good to be here. This is the first time I'm visiting this side of town and, man, it's even more gorgeous than my father's home village."

"I can almost smell the coconuts from here," said Derek with a hearty chuckle. "Enjoy your time off, brother. You deserve it. Your parents okay?"

"They're great. Retirement suits them very well and they've settled nicely in the village. How's Bali treating you and the fam?"

"Ah, it's paradise," Derek sighed contentedly. "You should see the kids splashing around in the pool, laughing and having a blast. It's moments like these that make everything worthwhile, you know?"

A flicker of envy stirred in Lucas's chest at the thought of Derek's family life, but he quickly stifled it. Instead, he focused on the lighthearted banter that came so naturally between them. "Yeah, well, maybe one day I'll find my own paradise."

"Who knows, maybe this visit will lead you to the woman of your dreams, Delgado. I haven't lost all hope for you, you know. Not yet, anyway."

"We'll see about that, Torreblanca, although you're beginning to sound like my parents. It's mildly disturbing."

"Hah! With good reason."

Lucas would have rolled his eyes had he not been driving

on his own. "Seriously, though, I've been meaning to ask. Do you think we're ready for a three-peat?"

"With you in top form? With Cordova at the helm? And with me keeping those overgrown Fil-Am kids off your back?"

The confidence in Derek's voice was overwhelmingly high. Lucas felt his hands tighten on the wheel at the thought of the upcoming Philippine Cup Conference—and their team's defense of the title for the second year in a row.

"I'll say we've got a very good chance," continued his friend. "So don't overthink it. We just need to stay focused and give it our all out there, just like before. What else can we do?"

Lucas took a deep breath, hoping he'd eventually have the same confidence at the end of his vacation. "I guess you're right."

"At my age, of course I'm right. But for now, you enjoy your time off, okay? Take care of yourself and give my regards to your parents."

"Thanks, man. You too. Say hi to Janice and hug the kids for me, will you?"

"Of course. Talk to you soon."

The call ended, leaving Lucas alone with his thoughts as he parked in front of the bungalow. Slowly, he stepped out of the car and unloaded his duffel bag from the back seat, careful not to shock his right knee at the change in position after many hours of driving.

He took a deep breath, welcoming the clean taste of the country air into his lungs. The balmy afternoon breeze was tinged with the distinct scent of orchids his mother loved, now carefully arranged in rows of driftwood that surrounded his parents' new home.

His mother, Mercy, was already standing on the porch with her arms outstretched to welcome him. She was a petite and elegant woman, with her gray hair cut short and neat. Age had made her lose none of the sharpness of her eyes; Lucas had believed since he was a child that he'd inherited his shooting proficiency from the sheer accuracy of his mother's gaze.

As soon as Lucas stepped onto the porch, she enveloped him in a tight embrace that seemed to defy her small frame. "I can't believe you're finally here!"

"Hello, Ma," he murmured into her hair, allowing himself to relish the familiarity of her presence.

"I've prepared the *tinola* you asked for," she said, patting him on the back. "And the village captain's wife sent some of her special pork *estopado*, too."

As they pulled apart, his father, Luis, came into view, stepping out into the waning afternoon light. A lanky, soft-spoken man with an artistic soul and a keen business mind, Luis had retired from his commercial ventures in the cities of Panay Island and now focused on assisting farmers in the province of Antique by investing in their cooperative efforts.

"Good to finally have you with us," Luis said warmly, clapping Lucas on the back as they exchanged smiles. "Hope you like the new place. We wanted something bigger for a possible cottage industry project with some local artisans. There's space here for that and more."

"Can't argue with that." From the wraparound porch, Lucas could see the stretch of farmland within his parent's property, bordered by a concrete-and-wire fence and rows of coconut trees. He gave a low whistle at the potential the space presented.

"Your father may have gotten the idea from the big coconut farm down the road," said his mother with a wry smile. "They've been making and exporting top-of-the-line food products for generations. Now he's thinking of expanding on that."

Luis nodded enthusiastically. "We're looking at coconut oil and soap, mats and ropes from fiber; and, of course, décor and accessories. People in this town already know how to make these products, so it's just a matter of harnessing those skills. That's what Galvez Farms did—and still does."

As he and his parents stepped into the spacious, airy bungalow, Lucas could practically hear the planning gears turning in his father's head as the older man spoke, but a familiar name quickly caught his attention. "Galvez?"

Mercy gestured for him to sit on the wooden dining table. An array of impressive-looking dishes were already laid out, among them a bowl of steaming chicken *tinola*, Lucas' favorite. "Yes, Galvez Farms is down the road from us, practically our next-door neighbor. You went to college with a Galvez who's now famous, didn't you? The singer?"

As hungry as he was from the long drive, the sumptuous

appearance and smell of the soup barely registered. All he could feel was a tight sensation in his throat as he attempted a coherent response. "You mean Tara? Tara Galvez?"

There was a strange glint in his mother's eyes as she took the seat from across his. "Ah, yes, Tara. She's the one who looks like an angel, doesn't she, Luis, from her pictures on the Internet? The new owner of the farm?"

His father, seated at the head of the table, nodded thoughtfully. "Yes, Tara Galvez. She bought out the farm from her parents and brothers not too long ago. Seems like Miss Galvez is taking a break from the city life, too, just like you. Heard about it from their foreman during the last town cooperatives meeting. She's supposed to be here now, but no one has seen much of her. The people here are very protective of the Galvez family."

"With good reason, I suppose," chimed in Mercy. "Galvez Farms practically put this entire town on the map with their coconut juice and preserves."

"That's true," Luis confirmed. "As far as I know, Miss Galvez wants to keep the farm and the business running. She's even asked the foreman to hire more workers from the neighboring villages to help during harvest season. Got some fancy folks from Iloilo City taking care of the books and exports, too. The farm seems to have doubled production over the past two years."

"Talented and clever young lady," declared his mother, giving Lucas a long, unblinking look before she continued. "Shall we say grace?"

His mother led a short prayer before she encouraged them to get started while the food was still hot. Lucas had clearly heard everything his parents just said, but the new information that swirled in his head was overpowered by a flood of memories from more than a decade ago.

Tara.

He'd first seen her standing next to a tree, a vision with pale skin and long black hair fluttering in the breeze, during basketball practice. She'd been watching him play, and he'd been unable to look away for so many long moments.

As fate would have it, she'd had his sketchbook with her. Lucas could recall picking her up, rain drenched and shivering, from the puddle on the campus grounds after she'd slipped trying to follow him. Tara Galvez had the most beautifully expressive and intelligent eyes he'd ever seen. By the time they'd reached the classroom for shelter, he was a goner. Later that evening, he'd walked her to the jeepney stop and given her his jacket to keep, but, in hindsight, he should have accompanied her home and never left her side.

He'd realized how special she really was when he read the poem she'd submitted, weeks later, to their college paper. As the illustrator for the publication, Lucas had felt a deep connection to her words, their meaning resonating as if she'd written the verses for him alone. Up until his final year at college, no matter how busy he was, he had never allowed anyone else to illustrate her poems.

Despite the undeniable pull he felt towards her, he never found the courage to talk to her again. He couldn't shake the fear that she would only see him as a shallow jock, incapable of appreciating the depth of her soul. By the time he finally mustered the resolve to approach her, it was too late—he was graduating and being drafted by a popular amateur basketball franchise, a mere step away from the country's premier league.

The idea of having Tara close by, *next door*…he could barely recall what he put into his mouth throughout dinner as his thoughts kept drifting, inexorably, back to her.

At the end of the meal, as they were tucking into small squares of *leche flan*, Lucas finally spoke. "I…I think I'd like to pay Miss Galvez—Tara—a visit. It's been so long, and I'd love to catch up."

"I think that's a wonderful idea," Mercy said warmly. "It would be nice to reconnect with someone from your college days while you're in town."

Lucas felt a flutter in his stomach as he replied. "Yeah, it would be great to see how she's doing. But I don't want to overwhelm her or anything. Maybe you've got some advice on the best time to visit her at Galvez Farms, Pa?"

Luis regarded him silently for a while before he answered. "Well, I know the foreman at the farm. He and his wife both work for Miss Galvez. They're all big fans of you and your team, too. He could give you some insight into when she might be available and what her schedule looks like."

"I'll prepare a basket of flowers and fruit for you to

bring," Mercy added. "You know, just to make it a little more special."

After dinner, his mother led him down the hallways of the bungalow for a quick tour, the polished wooden floors creaking softly beneath their feet. The soft lights in his parents' new home fell on walls adorned with family photographs and mementos—from the younger years of Lucas and his brothers, to pictures of grandchildren captured in various milestones. Mercy finally paused before a wooden sliding door, pushing it to reveal a generous space decorated with light earth tones.

"Here you are, Lucas. I hope it's comfortable enough for you."

"It's perfect, Ma." The bedroom was beautifully done, but it seemed larger than necessary for just one person. "Everything in this new place has plenty of room, I'll give you that."

"It always helps to be ready for a few more family members, don't you think?" His mother's eyes twinkled as she spoke. "Especially little ones. They'll need plenty of space to run around in."

He grinned at his mother's not-so-subtle hint. Both his older brother, who managed the family business of small supermarkets based in Iloilo City, and his younger brother, a surgeon who lived in Canada with his own family, had already fulfilled her dreams of a new generation of Delgados. Still, he sensed the underlying concern in her words.

"Slow down, Ma. You know I'm not even in a relationship right now. That might take a long while."

"It will take a long time, maybe never, if you keep hanging out with your showbiz lady friends." Mercy's teasing tone of voice was replaced by a more critical one. "Not such a good idea for a man your age."

He laughed it off, knowing that there was truth to her statement. "I know, Ma. Believe me, I can feel it in my bones. Literally."

His mother nodded seriously. She usually took his jokes in stride, but not this time. "You're not getting any younger, Lucas. It's time for you to find someone who truly understands you and your passions."

"With my kind of life, Ma, there are some things you have to put on pause."

"Well, then." Mercy squared her shoulders and made a move to exit the guestroom. "Whatever it is you decide, your father and I are already planning our Finals trip to Manila. A three-peat's not so far off, is it?"

Lucas smiled, grateful for her unspoken understanding of his situation and unwavering support for his chosen career. "Here's hoping. I'll tell Derek you said that, so he can work on his outside game during the training camp."

She nodded. "You do that. See you in the morning."

"Good night, Ma." He bent down to give her a hug and a quick peck on the cheek, before closing the door behind her.

Finally alone, he dropped his duffel bag onto the bed. He took a deep breath and allowed his posture to loosen, giving way to the tightness in his lower back that had bothered him since getting out of the car. His mother's words about his advancing age had hit him harder than he'd ever care to admit.

He knew it was only a matter of time before the secret was out, but that didn't mean he could still be as he was, if only for a little while longer. He could only hope to hold on long enough to finish the Philippine Cup Conference that year.

Lucas began to unpack the contents of his bag, his thoughts on Tara Galvez once more as he placed his clothes in the dresser. He had a collection of all her albums and singles, stashed away in his Manila apartment, hidden from the world on his bedside table.

As if on cue, his phone chimed with a notification, and he pulled it out to see that one of Tara's songs had been added to his Spotify playlist that had all her available music. He had watched her first live, sold-out performance online, all those years ago—a bootleg that he'd paid an exorbitant amount of money to acquire just so he could see her. Two years back, he had covertly attended one of her concerts, standing at the back of the crowd, too afraid to reveal himself but unable to stay away.

It was Tara who accompanied him during late-night drives after grueling practices or long games. The sound of her voice eased the burden of a career marked by losses and triumphs, trades and injuries. A life where much of reality was on pause, just as he'd said to his mother; a life where value and relevance depended on how much of a beating his body could take before it finally gave out.

Lucas scrolled through his phone's playlist and selected the song he wanted, the familiar delicate strumming of Tara's guitar filling the room as he sat on the bed. He closed his eyes as she began to sing, imagining her standing before him.

Lulled by her voice, he allowed his aching body to settle onto the pillows and drift off into a dreamless sleep.

My heart remembers you
Even if everything else doesn't

My love endures for you
Even if all else is gone

~ Excerpt from 'Gone'
Lyrics and music by Tara Galvez
Fragments of Us, Esta Melodia Records

CHAPTER 3

THE SUNSET

Tara

S HE SAT ON THE VILLA'S FRONT PORCH, STRUMMING HER guitar and scribbling down verses and notes as her mind raced to piece sound and feeling together. The weather was cooler today, Tara thought appreciatively, and lovelier to work outside in the fresh air for longer.

Just as she was about to start another verse, an unfamiliar voice cut through the stillness of the late afternoon.

"You stopped playing. I'm very sorry if I'm disturbing you." The voice was a deep baritone, male and seemingly sincere.

Her head snapped up, fingers stilling on the guitar

strings. Her heartbeat quickened, and for a split second, she wondered if she was experiencing some sort of vision or ghostly encounter.

Was it not only yesterday that she'd deemed him a memory locked away in her heart? Now, he stood on the top step, silhouetted by the fiery colors of the waning sun, an apologetic smile on his face.

"Lucas?" The name escaped her lips before she could stop herself.

"Hey, Tara. It's been a while, huh?"

It was Lucas Delgado, standing at the edge of her porch—the very real Lucas, whom she hadn't seen in person for over a decade.

The charming, lanky boy she'd met in college had now transformed into a towering figure, his lean, athletic build filling out his polo shirt and jeans effortlessly. His wavy black hair, stylishly layered to frame his handsome features, was slightly tousled by the wind. Time and age had changed him, molding him into someone who exuded confidence.

"Yeah, it's been a while." Tara swallowed, taking that one precious second to regain her composure. Steeling her nerves, she turned to face him, placing her guitar into its case on the coffee table. "What are you doing—I mean, what brings you here?"

His eyes had not changed. They were as dark and deep-set as she remembered, their corners crinkling as a bigger smile formed on his face, the familiar dimple forming on his right cheek.

"We're neighbors," Lucas said. "At least, you're neighbors with my parents, Luis and Mercy Delgado—I'm just a visitor. They bought a small farm and built their retirement home just down the road. My father had always wanted to live here. He grew up in the next village."

"I've heard about them. They've been helping and investing in cooperatives for a while now. I didn't know they were your parents."

"They're kind of low-key. It was my father who arranged for me to come to the farm and pay my respects. My parents spoke very highly of you. When they said it was *the* Tara Galvez who owned the farm next door, I had to see you."

She stared at him for a few long moments, before she recalled this was her domain—and she wasn't acting like it. She got to her feet and extended a hand. "I'm sorry. I wasn't expecting anyone at all. Welcome to Galvez Farms."

He shook his head and took her proffered hand. His grip was firm and warm, as reassuring as she remembered. "No. I should be the one to apologize for barging in unannounced. My father actually arranged for your foreman to escort me and make the introduction, but I managed to convince Fred to let me come up here on my own when I told him we knew each other from college."

She would have given anything to see Fred's face when the foreman met Lucas. "I couldn't blame him, to be honest. Everyone around here roots for your team."

"I'd happily take all the blame for this intrusion. I have

to admit I may have been a bit more pushy than usual. Please don't fire anyone. I'm a fan of yours, so it's on me."

The combined force of his touch and flattering words was enough to make the heat rush to her face. She let his hand go, trying to think of something weighty to say but finally settling on a simple truth. "It's okay. I trust the people here with my life."

He smiled, a mix of boyish sheepishness and gentle understanding. "So, does that mean I'm forgiven?"

"I'm not sure yet," came her measured response. "But it would be nice if you have a seat. Never let it be said I was rude to Lucas Delgado—or any of my neighbors, for that matter."

Lucas chuckled. "Fair enough. I brought you something from my mother's garden." He lifted a large basket off the top step and presented it to her with a small flourish. It was lined with red-and-blue checked cloth and filled with ripe yellow mangoes; a bouquet of white roses sat in the middle of the eye-catching arrangement. "She put this together for you. I hope you like it."

"It's very beautiful. Thank you." Tara accepted the offering, her fingers brushing against his. The contact sent an electric jolt up her arm, making her heart race. To disguise her flustered state, she glanced and gestured towards one of the rattan chairs. "Please make yourself comfortable."

She held the basket uncertainly, her hand still tingling from the brief contact with his. As Lucas settled into the chair, she added, "I have to admit, I didn't recognize you at first."

"Don't worry about it," he replied with a dismissive shake of his head and a reassuring smile. "It's been over a decade since we last saw each other, after all. I'm just glad you didn't mistake me for an intruder and bash me on the head with that beautiful guitar of yours. My face can't take any further damage."

She laughed at his self-deprecating humor, her anxiety at his unexpected appearance slowly fading. She decided to sit back down and was further relieved to see Marife, the head housekeeper of Galvez Farms, making her way to the porch.

"Good evening, Miss Tara," the older woman said, her eyes widening in surprise when she noticed Lucas. "Dinner will be ready soon."

"Fe, would you mind bringing some coconut juice for our guest?" Tara asked, grateful for the distraction. "Lucas, this is Marife. She looks after me here. You could say she runs the place. Fe, I'm sure you know Mr. Delgado."

She watched as Lucas stood up and introduced himself to the housekeeper, speaking to Marife with the same warmth and respect he had shown Tara moments ago.

No wonder Fred let him in unescorted, she mused, feeling a twinge of envy mixed with admiration.

As Marife bustled away to fetch the requested refreshment, Tara tried to focus on the present, resisting the urge to simply get lost in the moment without any word or explanation. She watched as the sunset made Lucas's bronzed skin glow, highlighting the thick waves of his hair.

"Thank you for the invitation to sit," he finally said,

breaking the silence that had settled between them. "It's so peaceful here."

"It's a very special place," she agreed. "The only place I could ever call home, really. I spent almost all my summers here until I graduated."

"I never knew." Lucas gazed at her with a faraway look in his eyes. "I spent a lot of time in the next village when I was younger. One of my uncles still has a house there. I'm surprised we never ran into each other."

"Well, we're here now," she offered.

"Perfect timing, I guess."

Before she could respond, Marife returned with glasses of fresh coconut juice.

As he sipped his drink, Lucas continued talking as if they weren't nearly strangers to each other. "Your music is fantastic, you know. I've always known you'll be great at it, since you first told me about it in college."

"Thanks," she mumbled. "I'm surprised you're familiar with my work."

"You've got such a unique sound, Tara. And those lyrics? *Wow.* Sometimes, it feels like you're singing just for me. It's incredible."

She found herself unable to meet his gaze. Instead, she shifted the conversation to safer ground. "So, how have you been? Do you still draw? You're so good at it."

He let out a small sigh. "Not really, no. I train almost all the time now, and when I do get a break, I'm usually preparing mentally for the next tournament. There just hasn't been much room for anything else, especially in the past few years."

The twinge of sadness in his voice tugged at her heart. She wanted to reach out to him, but could only manage a nod. "You've done a pretty great job for your team. It's never easy when you've got a lot of people counting on you."

"I'm surprised you're familiar with basketball," he replied, a smile in his voice.

"Championship trophies on the news and fashion billboards on Manila highways aren't exactly hard to miss," she retorted.

He raised an eyebrow. "I'm just glad no one managed to convince me to pose for the underwear line. That would have been a sight."

She wrinkled her nose. "Ew."

They shared a laugh, the sound making her even more comfortable in his presence. As the sound faded, so did the last rays of sunlight and more so the years that had separated them.

"Will you be staying at the village for some time, then? My parents mentioned they've heard you're taking a break from city life, just like me."

She hesitated, before finally deciding to let him know. "I've been here for more than a month now, working on my music for my next album. It will be my tenth anniversary in the industry at the end of the year, and I wanted to do something special." She paused, looking away for a moment. "Not many people know where I am, and I'd like to keep it that way."

To her surprise, he grinned in response. "Your secret is safe with me. In fact, I'll be your personal bodyguard while I'm here—protecting you from prying eyes and paparazzi. Least I could do after disturbing you earlier. And free of charge, of course." He winked, and Tara felt her cheeks redden at his comically roguish expression.

"Free of charge, huh?" she countered playfully. "Well, I suppose I could make an exception for such a generous offer."

"Please think about it and let me know." Lucas stood up, preparing to take his leave. "Thank you for the juice, and for your time. I'm really glad you're here, too. As I said, the timing couldn't have been more perfect."

He extended both hands with a gentle smile. She wondered if it was a double kind of handshake he was offering, or an attempt to hug her goodbye. But it was his face that really caught her attention.

He looked happy, content, and open—emotions she found herself wishing she could hold onto just a bit longer. Maybe, just this once, she could indulge herself.

With sudden resolve, the words left her mouth before she could second-guess them. "Would you like to stay for dinner? I usually eat alone. It would be nice to have some company for a change."

Her heart skipped a beat as she watched his smile widen. "I'd love to."

CHAPTER 4

THE JOURNEY

Lucas

NOTHING COULD HAVE PREPARED HIM FOR THE SHEER sight of her.

It was all he could do not to lose his composure at the beauty of Tara Galvez. She had a striking, ethereal look on her album covers and press photographs, but seeing her in person again was something else entirely.

"Do you mind if we go inside before it gets too dark?" She gestured to the wide, intricately carved sliding doors that led into the roomy, old-world villa. Even a simple question from her sounded like a song.

He nodded and watched her lean forward to zip up her

guitar case, unable to wipe the smile off his face as he did. She had a heart-shaped face, skin on the paler side, and expressive almond-shaped eyes framed by thick lashes. Her hair was a shimmering black, reaching down to the middle of her back.

As she made a move to lift the case, he extended a hand. "Let me get that for you."

Her gaze shifted to meet his, and he could feel his ribcage tighten at the effect of those eyes on him. He didn't need a whole team of overgrown Filipino-American players to stop him in his tracks; a look from Tara Galvez would be far more effective.

"Thanks," she said softly, turning on her heel. "Please, follow me."

"Lead the way." After picking up the guitar case, he reached for the basket of roses and mangoes with his other hand. As he straightened up, he tried to ignore the twinge of pain that shot up his lower back. Instead, he chose to focus on the woman before him.

When she walked, it looked like she was gliding on thin air. Combined with her stunning looks, the show business moniker for Tara, 'Asia's Acoustic Angel,' was more than fitting.

Upon entering the living room, Lucas noticed a framed, oddly familiar cut-out hanging on the wall. It took him a second or two to realize what it actually was.

It was Tara's first poem for their college paper, accompanied by his own illustration.

"Wow, I can't believe you still have this."

Standing next to him, she smiled softly. "Well, it was my grandmother who encouraged me to submit my poetry. She and my best friend, Jasmine, actually. They double-teamed me until I gave in."

"I'm glad they did," he replied, unable to help himself but smile at the basketball reference. He spied a yellowed photograph of an elegant couple a few frames to his left. Inching closer, he could see the gentleman's serious features, sleek dark hair, and sharp light-colored *barong*, the traditional Filipino men's shirt. Seated next to him, the lady had on a billowing dress, her hair piled high on her head. "Is that your grandmother?"

"Yes, with my grandfather." She moved to his opposite side, right in front of the portrait. "He used to be the singer of a four-piece *rondalla* back in the day. He gave me my first guitar. Since I was seven, we'd sing together during fiestas and special occasions."

"They look straight out of an old Sampaguita Pictures movie, don't they?"

"I used to think I'd never look as cool," Tara said fondly, her fingers caressing the edge of the frame. "I still do. I mean, c'mon. No one looks that good anymore."

"Well, it would be cool to recreate that photo like a lot of people do these days. I'd give anything to see you in that dress."

She raised an eyebrow at him. "Who'd be in that *barong*, then? You?"

"If it fits, who am I to say no to get a chance at looking like that? If you don't find me repulsive, of course."

She giggled, the sound reminding him of wind chimes. "You'll need kilos of pomade on your hair, for starters, but I think you'll make it work."

He could only stare, mesmerized at her laughter and her voice. He was willing to bet there was a matching grin on his face.

"Excuse me, Miss Tara? Dinner's ready."

His trance was broken by the soft, hesitant voice of Marife. He looked over his shoulder to see the older woman standing a few feet away.

"That's great," replied Tara. "Thanks, Fe."

As if on cue, a small parade of women flitted into the living room. With almost military-like precision, they switched on lights and insect repellent lamps, shut windows, and fastened screens against the encroaching night. It didn't escape him how many furtive glances they cast his way, punctuated by giggles and nudges. He responded politely, smiling and bidding each of the women a good evening. Two of them relieved him of the guitar case and the gift basket.

Marife ushered them through the living area and the wide archway that led to a vast dining room. The villa had smooth, shiny wooden floors and equally glistening pieces of carved mahogany furniture, each surface decorated with a basket or vase filled with white and yellow flowers. It was as if he had stepped into a different world, one of quiet intimacy, gentle beauty, and the calming yet beguiling presence of Tara Galvez.

"Please, sit down." Marife gestured to two set places of pearl-white china and polished silverware neatly arranged at one end of the long wooden table. Laid out before them was a lavish spread: the island's version of wonton soup called *pancit molo*, steamed duck with golden-brown sauce, grilled pork chops, and, of course, white rice. Further down, he could see a covered glass dish with familiar caramel-colored squares.

"Madam Mercy Delgado sent the *leche flan* for you, Miss Tara," said Marife, as if reading his mind. "She hopes you'll like it."

"They're my favorite. Best ever." He pulled out Tara's chair at the head of the table.

She rewarded him with a smile before sitting down. "Please thank your mother for me, Lucas. With her gift basket and now the dessert, I feel very spoiled."

"I'll be sure to," he replied as he took his own place to Tara's right. "Knowing her, she's just getting started."

Tara laughed lightly. "Fe, can you please make sure we send across one of our premium baskets to Mrs. Delgado first thing tomorrow?"

"Of course, Miss Tara."

"And thank you for this wonderful meal. I really didn't need anything this grand."

"Of course you do, Miss Tara," Marife replied, her tone firm yet affectionate. "You deserve nothing less."

They watched as the other women trailed into the dining room bearing drinks. One placed a pitcher of ice-cold coconut juice before them, while another set down wineglasses and a bottle of red.

"From your grandfather's collection, Miss Tara. With Sir Lucas as our guest, I thought you would want to serve the *tempranillo*."

Lucas caught the eye of the women, winking playfully. "Thank you for taking such good care of Tara—and of me, of course. I hope this won't be the end of your generosity." They responded with titters and blushing nods before quietly dispersing under Marife's discreet prompting.

"Thank you, ladies," murmured Tara. "Good night."

Marife surveyed the table with a practiced eye. "Will you be needing anything else, Miss Tara?"

"I'm fine, thank you, Fe," she responded. "Lucas?"

He grinned at Marife. "I've got everything I need right here, Fe. Thanks."

They both bid the older woman good night and watched as she exited the room, finally leaving them alone. As the last remnants of daylight faded behind the curtains of the villa, he was glad to see Tara settle more comfortably around him, pouring wine and encouraging him to eat more of their delicious meal. He asked her questions about her music and concerts, watching as she spoke animatedly about her experiences on the road, performing in different cities and countries.

"Sometimes it's surreal, to think that my music has

reached a lot of people and touched so many lives. It's both humbling and inspiring. Still can't believe it most of the time." Tara took a sip of her wine and tipped her glass in his direction. "And what about you? You're always on the move, too."

"I've found my own way, I suppose," he responded, shifting slightly in his seat to ease the discomfort in his right knee at being seated for a while. "Learned to adapt to being on the road most of the time. I was lucky to get traded to my team six years ago. They've become like family to me now."

Lucas watched as she listened intently as he spoke, longing to tell her it was her music that had been his constant companion, over and above the people around him. The hours passed effortlessly as they shared stories and laughter about their travels. The plates before them emptied and the night deepened, but he didn't care. Just as he'd said earlier, he had all he ever wanted with him, right there in that dining room.

It was a surprise when the clock struck midnight. Tara glanced at the antique carved grandfather in a corner of the dining room, the surprise flickering in her eyes mirroring his own. "I can't believe it's so late already."

"Happens when you're in good company," he replied honestly, unable to shake the feeling that their time together was too short. He knew he had to see her again.

"I should walk you to the door," she said as she got to her feet. "You drove here, didn't you?"

He nodded as he stood up. "My car's parked just outside the gates. Walked in with Fred, but then…you know."

He followed her as she made her way back to the living room, careful not to show any signs of his lower back protesting or his knee going partially numb after hours of being off his feet.

She looked over her shoulder with a smile. "I know. Guess it all turned out okay." Perhaps it was the effect of the smooth, decades-old *tempranillo*, but he could see a pinkish tint on her cheeks.

"It did." He paused just before they reached the front door, his heart pounding. He felt like a schoolboy again, mesmerized and dumbstruck at the mere sight of a beautiful girl.

"It was very nice of you to visit," she said, extending a hand. "This evening has been wonderful."

"Thank you for having me." He shook her hand and leaned down to press a quick peck on her cheek. "It's an honor to be with you, Tara."

The warmth of her skin beneath his lips was sweet and welcoming, carrying the scent and taste of vanilla and coconuts. Unable to help himself, he wrapped his arms around her.

She hugged him back, her arms going up and around his torso slowly. The embrace was awkward at first, but they soon relaxed into each other.

It was Tara who pulled away first. "Good night, Lucas," she said softly.

"Good night." He stepped through the threshold, allowing her to close the door between them. He turned to leave, but as he took his first step down the porch, a surge of hope welled up within him, and he couldn't resist turning back.

"Can I visit again tomorrow? I could keep you company, be your bodyguard while you work on your music."

Still standing on the doorway, she hesitated, her smile wavering for a moment before she finally nodded in agreement. "I'd like that."

A sudden rush of joy coursed through him, a giddy sensation of excitement at the prospect of spending more time with her. As he waved goodbye and walked off into the night, he found that, for the first time in a long while, the pain in his body no longer weighed so heavily.

What mattered now was the promise of tomorrow, as something akin to hope bloomed within his heart.

I was the one
Who looked at you
From across the room
The one who felt your pain
And never gave it back
I cared not
If you can't even see
Just in dreams
Be with me

I was the one
You looked right through
I was part of you
That shudder in the hall
That whisper at the moonless sky
That gaze on your back
That one
Loving you

~ Excerpt from 'That One'
Lyrics and music by Tara Galvez
Fragments of Us, Esta Melodia Records

CHAPTER 5

THE KISS

Tara

BEING IN THE GARDEN HAD ALWAYS BROUGHT HER A sense of tranquility, but today she couldn't shake the feeling that she was on the brink of something new and unknown.

Tara carefully plucked each golden blossom from its stem, her fingers brushing against the soft petals as she filled a basket woven from coconut leaves. With the white roses Lucas' mother had sent yesterday, she envisioned harmonious arrangements she could create throughout the house. It was a project that would hopefully distract her from thoughts of the very man himself.

Or from thoughts of his little kiss last night, and the way he'd put his arms around her for the first time.

Where is he?

She felt a slight shift in the breeze and looked up to see the foreman of Galvez Farms, Fred, approaching her with a hesitant smile, his hat clutched to his chest. Together with his wife, Marife, they had served the farm for more than three decades.

Ageless, sun-browned, and usually sprightly, he looked almost drawn as he stopped a few feet away, eyes downcast. "Good morning, Miss Tara."

She put her basket aside and got to her feet, dusting her hands and sliding off her gloves. "Good morning, Fred. Everything okay?"

He slowly raised his eyes to meet hers, shaking his head ruefully. "I shouldn't have let Mr. Delgado come to the villa alone yesterday. I mean, I know his parents…and he told me he knew you from college and he's your biggest fan. I don't know what came over me. I'm so sorry, Miss Tara."

At the back of her mind, a gentle reprimand would be suitable, but all she felt was a light-hearted sensation bubbling up from within her at the mention of Lucas' insistence.

"Don't worry about it," she replied with what she hoped was a reassuring smile. "I know you're a big fan of his, and so is everyone else in the village. It's not the first time someone's been star-struck."

"Still, I should have been more careful," Fred mumbled. "Your safety is very important."

"It's not a problem. Just be more careful next time, okay?" As the words left her mouth, she realized she hadn't felt intruded upon by Lucas' presence. In fact, it seemed as if he belonged right there, with her.

"Okay, Miss Tara." The foreman hesitated for a moment, before he continued, "Do you want me to put in extra hours? Or maybe you wanna cut my pay for the month?"

"What? No! Why would I do that?" She shook her head, amusement and exasperation warring within her. "Really, Fred. It's alright, I promise."

"If you say so."

"I say so. Now, please, don't worry about it."

Just as Fred was about to take his leave, the sound of approaching voices drew her attention to the garden path. Marife was walking towards them with none other than Lucas Delgado in tow. Even in the distance, his tall silhouette was unmistakable, making her heart beat a little faster at the memory of his lips, soft and damp, on her cheek.

"Good morning, Miss Tara." The housekeeper's round face was all aglow as she grinned up at the man next to her. "I met Sir Lucas at the gate on my way back from the market. He asked if I could let him in."

Lucas greeted Tara with a warm smile. "Good morning, Tara. Hope it's okay."

"Good morning," she managed to reply, trying to maintain her composure despite the heat that suffused her cheeks. "Of course it's okay."

"Hey, Fred," Lucas called over to the foreman, who

remained rooted to the spot, still clearly star-struck. "I was thinking, maybe it's time for you to replace that old motorbike of yours. I spoke to someone from the village cooperative earlier today and they'll help coordinate the purchase for me. You know Dodie, don't you? Talk to him for me, okay?"

Fred and Marife stared at him, their eyes widening in shock. It was Marife who recovered first. With a squeal, she hugged Lucas tightly, jumping up and down like an overjoyed child. Her husband followed suit, more slowly but no less joyously.

Lucas patted them both on their backs, shrugging off their nearly incoherent words of gratitude with a smile. "It's the least I could do."

Tara found herself speechless as she watched the awkward, sweet exchange, deeply touched by Lucas' thoughtfulness and the ease with which he endeared himself to those around her.

"Anyway, I brought something for you." Once he was no longer in the group hug, Lucas turned his attention to her, holding up a brown bag. The freshly-baked aroma that wafted from the bag made her mouth water instantly. "It's *pan de sal*. I went to the next village first thing before they're all sold out. I hope I'm not intruding too early in your day."

"No, your timing is perfect," she said, mirroring his words from the night before, warmth spreading through her chest as she took in his easy smile.

Lucas' eyes twinkled, but before he could respond, Marife and Fred thanked him profusely once more, fussing over him one last time before they excused themselves, mumbling about their respective duties in the farm.

"Thank you." It was all she could say as soon as the couple was out of earshot. "That's very kind of you."

"My father called Fred yesterday morning, asking if he could arrange for me to visit the farm. He picked me up from my parents' house in his motorbike. While he was bringing me up here, we talked a bit about his family. I thought it would help a little if he had a new motorbike. I'm really grateful he made this happen…you know, getting me into the farm so I could see you."

Tara's heart pounded at his candid declaration, unable to understand why such a simple act could mean so much to him.

Lucas gave her a gentle smile as he continued. "You know, there was a time when I thought I'd give anything just to be with you up close. And now, here I am, standing in this beautiful place with you. Still feels like a dream."

It was her turn to get dumbstruck. Was this really happening, or have all the months in near isolation, with only her music for company, made her go crazy? Was this really Lucas Delgado, the very heart of every story told in her songs?

"Are you okay?" There he stood before her, concern etched on his face.

She nodded quickly, wanting to steer the conversation away from the intensity of the moment. "I don't usually have breakfast, but the bread you've brought smells incredible. I think I have the perfect coffee to go with it."

She was relieved to see his concerned expression get quickly replaced by a smile.

"That's great because this *pan de sal* is said to be the best in the entire province, maybe even the whole country." Lucas carefully took a piece of bread from the bag and, instead of handing it to her, brought it to her lips.

Tara felt lightheaded as she took a bite, savoring the flavor that seemed to be enhanced by his touch.

"Is it good?"

"Yes," she replied, knowing she was blushing, but unable to tear her gaze away from him. "It's wonderful."

"Another bite?" The teasing lilt in his voice made her blush deepen.

She nodded, her heart pounding so loudly she could barely hear anything else around them. "Please."

He brought the bread to her lips once more, and she eagerly took another bite. As he pulled the bread away, his thumb brushed against the corner of her mouth, flicking off a stray crumb. The slight contact made her shiver in the morning sun, his touch leaving her feeling both exposed and exhilarated.

"Oops, I missed another one." With a playful smile, he bent down and brought his lips to the corner of her mouth. His tongue teased the sensitive skin, causing her breath to catch in her throat.

She wasn't entirely sure if there was even a crumb there in the first place, but in that instant, she couldn't bring herself to care. All she knew was that her hands had somehow found their way to his shirt, gripping the fabric tightly, holding on as if she was about to get swept away. The bag of bread slipped from his grasp, forgotten as it tumbled to the ground and rolled into a patch of vibrant flowers.

His lips slid effortlessly to fully meet hers, moving lazily, as if exploring something delicate and precious. He paused for a moment, pulling back just enough to murmur, "Is this okay? Am I intruding?"

Without hesitation, she replied, "No, your timing is perfect." As if to further emphasize her point, she wound her arms around his neck and drew him closer. It struck her then just how tall he truly was, yet he seemed to have no trouble bending to meet her level.

As the kiss grew increasingly passionate, she became dimly aware that he had lifted her off the ground, her back almost pressed against the rough bark of a nearby coconut tree, cushioned only by his hand. She wrapped her legs around his hips, the sensation of his arms around her body further fueling her desire.

His free hand roamed over her, fingers tracing the delicate lines of her collarbone and shoulders. She reveled in his touch, allowing a moan to escape her lips, as her own hands tangled in his thick hair, tugging as she ground herself against him.

"God, you're so beautiful," Lucas groaned into her ear, his breath hot and urgent. "So wonderful…Are you even real?"

His words, spoken with such awe and disbelief, sent a jolt through Tara, pulling her back from the edge of abandon.

"Wait," she breathed out, a wave of self-doubt taking over as she placed a hand on his chest, a plea for pause.

Instantly, he stilled, his broad shoulders heaving as he came up for air. Though the heat of passion still smoldered in his eyes, it was tempered by concern.

"Sorry," she whispered. "I just need to… I want to take my flowers inside before they dry out."

Without a word, he nodded as he carefully set her back down on the ground. He stepped back, giving her space, while absently helping her straighten her clothes.

Almost reluctantly, he separated himself from her. He looked away as he picked up the bag of bread and basket of flowers, extending both to her. "Do you want me to go?"

Instead of answering him directly, she asked, "Would you like to stay for breakfast? There's too much bread here for just me."

"I'd love to." He smiled tentatively and adjusted his grip, extending a free arm towards her. "Shall we?"

Tara nodded and hooked her arm through his. Together, they made their way back to the villa with unhurried steps. Nothing further was said between them, but the real, burning question lingered in her mind.

What did she really want?

CHAPTER 6

THE GARDEN

H E WONDERED WHAT SHE WAS THINKING, HOW SHE felt about their stolen moment in the garden, but he knew better than to ask.

Instead, Lucas chose to focus his attention on carrying the brown bag of *pan de sal* and her basket of golden flowers in one hand, while Tara held on to his other arm. At the corner of his eye, she looked seemingly lost in thought.

"This place is even more magical in the morning," he said as they reached the top of the porch steps. "It feels so serene, doesn't it?"

"Thanks," Tara replied softly, her voice barely audible

as she let go of his arm upon reaching the threshold. "I've always loved it here in the mornings, when it's not yet too warm in the day."

She offered to make fresh coffee and led him to a large kitchen further inside the house. As soon as they entered the sunny room that seemed to occupy the entire back of the villa, she immediately busied herself, instructing him to put the bag and basket on the counter. As she worked, he stood near the windows, taking in the sprawling view of the coconut farm.

"Would you like to have breakfast outside?" Her eyes met his for the briefest of moments before darting away. She gestured to a small balcony built into the corner of the kitchen. "My grandparents used to eat there in the mornings."

"Sounds perfect."

"Please go ahead. I'll be with you in a minute."

He complied and took a seat on one of the wooden chairs. Before him, Galvez Farms extended as far as the eye could see, coconut trees waving gently in the breeze, while a smattering of birdsong provided a soothing, dreamy soundtrack. He could feel the tension and aches in his body slowly ebbing away at the peaceful scene.

She joined him minutes later, carrying a wooden tray with a pot of coffee and a plateful of bread. She seemed to relax as well, her shoulders softening as she took in the view.

As they drank and ate in silence, she would occasionally glance at the *pan de sal* in her hand, her cheeks flushing with color before she quickly turned away. He pretended not to notice, focusing a little too intently on his own drink and food.

"Your parents have been doing great work for the community," Tara said, after they had emptied the pot of coffee and almost finished all the bread.

Lucas nodded, grateful for the chance to steer their conversation towards a safe topic. "Yeah, they're really dedicated to helping out. My dad's always been passionate about giving back, especially to places like this. He taught me and my brothers how important it is to invest in local communities."

Tara's eyes lit up. "My grandparents started their export business years ago by partnering with locals to harvest coconuts and produce world-class juices and canned goods. They believed in supporting our people and our culture."

"My mother mentioned the other day it was Galvez Farms that put this town on the map. That's some legacy you got there."

"My family and I do our best," she replied with a smile. "Since I was a little girl, I've dreamt of having a place like this."

"And now you do."

She nodded, her gaze sweeping the scenery before them. "Still can't believe it sometimes, you know."

He took in the unguarded look of adoration on her face as she spoke, knowing he would give anything—do anything—for her to look at him the same way.

Silence came over them once more, but this time it didn't feel as charged or heavy.

"By the way, my mother has invited you for lunch at the

house this Sunday after Mass. The service will be at the village chapel, so you won't have to worry about prying eyes. My father and some of the other men will be there to make sure everything is okay." He tried to sound casual, trying to ignore the cold sweat he felt popping up at the back of his neck.

"Really? That sounds lovely. I haven't been to the village in such a long time. I'd be honored to come."

"That's great." Relief coursed through him, paired with a sense of gratitude towards his parents. "She'll be thrilled."

"I need to come up with something for your mother to thank her for her gifts yesterday," she said, a thoughtful look on her face. "I think I ate four of those mangoes after you went home last night—and all the *leche flan*, too."

A chuckle escaped him at the thought of her hearty appetite. "That's won't be necessary. Just having you there would be gift enough for my parents. They're looking forward to meeting you after I confirmed you really were *the* Tara Galvez I knew from college."

That was the understatement of the year. Earlier that day, even before the sun had risen, his parents had grilled him about the previous night's events. From the look of joy on their faces, he knew they were already planning for future grandchildren. His mother was now probably mentally redecorating the guest room for a family, never mind the old bachelor who stayed in it.

Tara shook her head. "No, I insist. I'll make *biko* using my grandmother's recipe. I've got signed copies of my two albums, too."

"Alright, you win," he relented, secretly pleased at her insistence. "Go for it, then."

"Good. I'll be making the *biko* today, and you'll be helping me."

After they cleared away the dishes from the balcony, she led him to the living room. He hadn't noticed it earlier, but on top of the coffee table was a hamper overflowing with an assortment of drawing materials.

"These belonged to my grandmother," Tara explained in a soft, almost reverent voice. "She would use them to design dresses for me and the other village girls during the May *Santacruzan* parades. Go ahead, take a look."

Lucas gently sifted through the contents of the basket: well-loved colored pencils, delicate pastel chalks, and thick paper either loose or ring-bound into sketchbooks. He could barely remember where his own drawing materials were, if there were any left; years had passed since he'd last sketched anything.

"Thanks," he blurted out against the tightness forming in his throat. "You didn't have to…"

"I don't want you to be bored while you're here. I thought these might help keep you entertained. You said yesterday it's been a while since you drew something. Besides, the Wi-Fi in the farm is a little kooky and often unreliable."

He laughed. "You're right. This seems to be the perfect time to start drawing again, especially with you around. One piece of poetry from you and—boom!—I'll be drawing like a pro in no time."

"I guess you can look at some of my lyrics," she offered. "In strict confidence, of course."

He nodded, his eyes never leaving hers. "Everything seems to be perfectly timed for us, isn't it?"

She blushed and mumbled a response, her gaze flitting away. Sensing her discomfort, he decided not to push the matter further. Instead, he focused on her presence, following her around the house as she gathered together ingredients and utensils for the *biko*.

Just before lunchtime, she had him stirring the mixture of sticky rice, coconut milk, and brown sugar over the stove, supervising with a keen eye as she spoke of memories making the dish.

"Every time we made this, I remember my grandmother teaching me how to get the consistency just right. She'd say that the secret was in the wrist, but I think it was really in her heart."

Lucas smiled as he listened to her reminisce, marveling at how easily they fell into a familiar rhythm. Tara's approval of his cooking skills came soon after; she declared that the *biko* was perfect and only final touches were needed before she put it away to 'set.' She proceeded to drizzle calamansi juice and toasted coconut shavings on top of the rich brown rice cake before packing it up in a covered glass dish lined with banana leaves.

Lunch passed in a blur, with Marife and the other women beaming at him meaningfully before bustling away. When the afternoon arrived, Lucas found himself settling into a comfortable chair on the front porch, his inherited sketch-pad in hand, while Tara strummed her guitar and hummed melodies to herself, pausing to jot down on her notebook.

Dinner came and went just as quickly, with a spread as equally generous as the previous evening's. This time, Tara didn't protest at the lavish selection of dishes set out before them.

As midnight approached, he reluctantly stood up from the table, knowing it was time to leave. "Thanks, Tara. It's been a wonderful day. Can't think of a better way to end it."

She smiled warmly at him as she got to her feet. "I agree. It's been perfect."

He followed her to the front door. Before he could step out into the night, he remembered the drawing he had completed that afternoon. He retrieved the loose piece of paper nestled within his sketchbook, which he'd carefully stashed away on a side table in the living room. "I wanted to show you this before I left."

The illustration was of Tara, in her light-colored shirt and jeans, black hair flowing in the breeze, standing amidst beds of white and gold flowers, surrounded by the cool shadows of coconut trees. He presented it to her, suddenly feeling shy.

Her wide eyes and soft gasp were affirmation enough. "Oh my god, this is…it's beautiful. You drew me exactly how I felt this morning—peaceful, alive, content."

"Thanks," he replied, his cheeks warming at her praise. "It had better be beautiful when I'm drawing such a beautiful sight."

Without another word, she stepped forward and wrapped her arms around him. He hugged her back gently, careful not to push her like he had during their kiss that morning.

"Good night, Lucas," she murmured into his shirt.

He pressed a kiss to the top of her head, inhaling the pure and sweet yet deliciously enchanting vanilla scent of her. "Can I see you again tomorrow? I hope I've been a good bodyguard today."

She giggled as she pulled back, reaching over to squeeze his hand. "Yes, you've been excellent. You make a great *biko*, too, so that counts. You're hired."

With one last look into her eyes, he turned and walked away. This time, she watched him go, calling out goodbye just before he lost sight of her and the villa.

Suddenly on his own without her, he was left with a feeling of emptiness and loss as he made his way through the night.

If only I could have a moment
I would stop time
To be with you
If only I could live in dreams
Then I would fly to you

All these could never be
Yet I won't stop loving you

~ Excerpt from 'Afar'
Lyrics and music by Tara Galvez
Fragments of Us, Esta Melodia Records

CHAPTER 7

THE MEMORY

Tara

THE EARLY AFTERNOON SUN WAS WARM ON HER FACE as Lucas drove from the village chapel to the Delgado house. On the front seat, Tara looked outside the window, focusing on the sights of vibrant greenery and distant mountains before her.

She tried not to think of her nerves at seeing his parents again after meeting them before Mass earlier that day. Mercy and Luis Delgado had been very charming, but the way they would look at her and then at Lucas in quick succession, then exchanged smiles, she expected them to eventually ask questions.

As they pulled up to a bungalow with a wraparound veranda covered by a colorful assortment of orchids, she knew they had reached their destination. Seconds later, Mercy hurried out, a big smile on her face. Lucas gave her a sheepish smile before she stepped out of the vehicle to greet his mother.

"Welcome to our home, Tara. I told Lucas we simply must have you over." The older woman embraced her tightly as soon as she stepped onto the porch, and Tara hugged her right back.

Holding her at arm's length, Mercy continued, "Oh my goodness, you are even more beautiful in person. You really do look like an angel."

She blushed at the gushing compliment, lowering her head. "Uh, thanks, Mrs. Delgado."

"Mercy, please, dear."

"Ma, you're embarrassing her," Lucas said, grinning as he made his way around the SUV to join his father at the doorway.

"Let your mother be, Lucas," Luis admonished his son playfully. Turning to Tara, he added, "You should know by now that between Lucas and his brothers, a young lady like yourself is a very welcome addition to our family."

"Pa!" Lucas choked on nothing, his ears turning red as Tara suppressed a giggle, her own embarrassment momentarily forgotten. Mercy, however, was not as amused, and she swiftly elbowed her husband in the ribs, who tried to muffle a pained grunt.

"Sorry, dear," Luis muttered, rubbing his side. "I just meant to say that we are very happy to have you here, Tara."

"Thank you, Mr. Delgado…uh, Luis."

"That's better," said Mercy approvingly, taking her hand. "Come on, Tara. I'm sure you're hungry."

She nodded gratefully, allowing herself to be swept up in the gentle rhythm of the Delgado family's affection and care. The home of Lucas' parents was filled with natural light, its walls adorned with lovingly arranged photos and framed diplomas.

After taking her on a quick tour around the bungalow, Mercy led her to the cozy dining room. As she sat down to join them, she felt a sense of belonging, at being welcome without expectation or demand. She suddenly missed her own parents, who both still lived in her childhood home in Iloilo City, at the other end of the island.

After grace, Mercy served bowls of home-cooked native chicken *tinola*, saying it was Lucas' favorite, and generous slices of *lechon*, which, Luis said proudly, was cooked by the village men themselves.

"Best food in town, equaled only by the five-star dining experience at Galvez Farms," Lucas commented, giving an enthusiastic thumbs-up. Seated next to Tara, he obediently finished whatever his mother served to him. "Keep this up, Ma, and I might never want to leave."

"Here, have some more, Tara." Mercy reached over and slid a few more slices of crispy *lechon* skin onto Tara's plate.

"Well, that's the plan, isn't it? What do you think, dear, is he worth keeping around?"

She swallowed before looking up from her food, only to feel herself redden as her eyes met Lucas'.

"He's a great bodyguard and very resourceful at getting nice food," she offered hesitantly. "He can also make *biko* from scratch. I guess he'll be quite useful to have around."

The expectant expressions of everyone around the table turned to mirth, Mercy's merry laugh joined by the deeper, almost harmonizing chuckles of her husband and son.

As the conversation rose and fell around her, Tara savored each mouthful of food, allowing the flavors to transport her back to those simpler summer days spent with her grandparents. When dessert was served—a rich, creamy-green *buko pandan*—her nostalgic bubble gave way to a burst of emotion as the familiar taste flooded her senses.

"Are you okay?" Lucas reached out and gave her hand a quick squeeze.

She nodded, a lump forming in her throat as she tried to give voice to her memories. "*Buko pandan* was my grandfather's favorite. He had it every Sunday, too."

Mercy smiled affectionately. "I made these with the ingredients from the basket you sent with Marife last week. I hope you like it."

Tara looked around the table with what she hoped was a reassuring smile. "I love it. It's really wonderful. It's…" To her horror, a lone tear slid out from the corner of her eye.

"Excuse me," she muttered, pushing back her chair.

She took a few unsteady steps away from the table, not daring to look at the faces of her hosts, before making her way to the living room. She settled on the sofa, taking deep, measured breaths as a few more tears rolled down her cheeks. She willed herself to get it together—breaking down like this was humiliating.

"Hey." Lucas crouched down before her, peering up at her face with concern in his eyes. She didn't realize he had followed her. "Are you alright?"

"Yeah," she mumbled. "I just needed a minute."

"My parents could come on a little too strong sometimes. Sorry about that."

She shook her head. "Your family has been nothing but kind to me."

He slowly stood up and seated himself next to her. She could have sworn she saw him grit his teeth, but the sight was gone just as quickly, replaced by his usual smile. "Have I done something wrong, then?"

She shook her head again, wiping at her eyes with the back of her hand.

"Shall I take you home? Or we can drive down into town if you'd like a change of scenery. I've got to be back at six, though. I'm playing in the fund-raising game between the junior and senior high school teams."

"No, no, it's fine. I'm fine, really."

He reached into his pocket and held out a maroon checked handkerchief, using his other hand to lift her chin. "Sure?"

"Really, Lucas—"

"Sure?" He goggled at her like a puppy dog, blinking furiously.

She giggled and sniffled as she swatted him on the upper arm. "Don't be silly."

He tickled her chin before letting go, eliciting a smile from her as she dabbed at her eyes with his handkerchief. "That's more like it."

A sigh escaped her as she felt her body relax; she found herself half-leaning against his body. His arm went around her shoulders as if it was the most natural thing in the world for him to do.

"It's the *buko pandan*," she confessed. "It tasted exactly like the one in my memories—the one my grandmother used to make every Sunday. It tasted like…home."

She could feel tears once again welling up behind her eyes, but she blinked hard and chose instead to focus on the man holding her. Lucas smelled of the cologne that he endorsed; clean and sharp, with lemony notes.

"Home, huh?" he echoed, his voice pitched so low it was a rumble in his chest.

"Yeah…I'm sorry for being such a crybaby. I should apologize to your parents."

"No, you don't have to."

She shook her head and made a move to stand up, but he grabbed her hand to stop her.

"Tara, wait."

She hesitated before she slowly eased herself back onto the sofa. "What?"

He reached for her cheek this time, gently coaxing her to look in his direction. She obliged; when she looked into his eyes, she immediately knew what she saw in them would forever change her.

"Maybe you are home," he said quietly. "Maybe you are home with me."

CHAPTER 8

THE GAME

Lucas

H E KNEW ONCE HE UTTERED THE WORDS THERE WAS NO turning back.

Home. That was the feeling.

He was simply adrift on a sea of existence when they were apart—and only ever alive when she was with him. The realization was both blinding in its simplicity and overwhelming in its magnitude.

Tara's eyes widened, her face coloring furiously. It was all he could do not to take her into his arms and kiss her breathless, never mind that his parents were in the next room.

"I…I don't understand," she breathed. "Lucas, I—"

"A-hah! There you two are!"

Before she could finish, Luis appeared at the doorway, straightening his glasses. If he had seen or heard anything, it didn't really show on the smile on his face. "We thought you wanted her all to yourself, Lucas, and spirited her away."

"I'm sorry for running out like that," said Tara. "I felt a little dizzy."

"Are you okay now, dear?" Mercy walked up to the doorway, too, and made her way into the living room. "Would you like to lie down for a bit?"

Tara shook her head as she gave his parents a reassuring smile, clearly a little awkward under their scrutiny. "Thank you. I'm fine now."

"We were just talking about tonight's game, Ma." Lucas smoothly took over the conversation as his parents settled into comfortable chairs next to them. "In fact, Pa, maybe you'd like to ask Tara what you mentioned to me the other day?"

"It's for a good cause, of course," said Luis. "The kids want to raise some money for their libraries and canteens. The high school really took a hit from the typhoon last November. We were thinking it might be nice if you'd perform a song during halftime, Tara."

"That's something that would inspire a lot of people," Mercy added gently.

"Really?" Tara looked taken aback by the suggestion. She turned to him, perhaps for support, but glanced away just as quickly. "I don't know, Luis…this is a surprise, for sure."

"Inspire is right, though," Lucas commented, clearly aware

he was speaking from personal experience. "It would be the perfect morale booster for everyone here."

"We'll make sure no one announces your appearance beforehand," his father assured her. "Lucas did mention how you wanted keep your privacy. We'll keep all the buzz to a minimum."

"I'll be there the whole time," Lucas added. "I'll still be on bodyguard duty, if you promise you'll watch me play." He finished with a wink at her, hoping the lighthearted gesture would put her at ease.

She only stared at him doubtfully. "It's been a while since I performed, Lucas…"

"Please?" he interjected. "As your biggest fan, I can say for certain you'll be fantastic."

"One song, dear." His mother reached over and patted Tara's hand. "Why don't you sing that truly heartbreaking ballad of yours, the one where there's a part that says 'be happy'? It's on the radio all the time. I believe the video has that really handsome actor, Paolo something? No, it's Pio-"

"'Never with You,'" said Tara quietly.

"Ah, yes, that's the one. Beautifully written, so haunting, don't you think so, Lucas?"

He nodded in agreement. "What do you say, Tara?"

"Alright," she agreed, her voice soft, almost drowned out by the excited reactions of his parents. "I'll do it."

"Fantastic!" Luis was already on his feet, reaching for his phone in his back pocket. "Everyone will be thrilled to hear your beautiful voice in person, Tara. I know we all are."

"You'll be so awesome," Lucas assured her. "We'll help you get ready, won't we, Pa?"

"Anything you need, anything at all. Just let us know." With the cool-headed control of a seasoned business leader, his father immediately went into planning mode with the game's organizers.

The rest of the afternoon passed by in a flurry of enthusiastic activity, the anticipation for Tara's performance palpable in the air. Marife was at the house by four o'clock with Tara's guitar. The Galvez housekeeper also brought a simple white dress and sandals, which Mercy happily received.

He and Tara crossed paths in the hallway, with her being led into the other guestroom by his mother to get ready, while he was on his way out of the house, his gear already in tow.

"I'm really excited to hear you sing tonight." He reached for her hand and gave it a tight, reassuring squeeze. "I know you'll be great."

"Thanks." To his surprise, she clung to his hand. At the corner of his eye, he could see his mother discreetly striding down the hallway to the guestroom, giving them privacy.

"You okay?"

"Yeah. Are you…I mean, will you be going with me to the game?"

"I'm actually going earlier with my father, to talk to the teams and warm up with them. The driver will take you and my mother to the high school gym just before six."

Her face fell. "Oh. I see."

"If you want, I can ask my father to go ahead without me."

Wide-eyed, she shook her head. "You've got to be there. Spend time with those kids. It's not every day they get to play with you on their team."

He grinned and raised her hand to his lips, pressing a light kiss to her knuckles. "I guess you're right. It's still an honor to be asked to play for a team, any team. Never outgrew that feeling."

She smiled, a little hesitantly. "I'll see you later, then. Good luck."

"See you later." As was their routine, he bent down to hug her goodbye. Instead of putting her arms around his torso like she usually did, she used the collar of his shirt to pull him down for a quick kiss on the lips.

The contact was over just as quickly, but he knew it happened—the hot brand of her lips on his, the lingering scent of her hair and skin. Most of all, his entire body jolted and stiffened, as if he'd been electrocuted.

If they were alone, things would turn out very differently.

Instead, he adjusted the strap of his sports bag higher on his shoulder and reluctantly let her go. With a final glance and quick wave over his shoulder at Tara, Lucas joined his father, who was waiting on the porch.

The violent, giddy pounding of his heart never stopped, not even when he drove off, not even when they reached the high school gymnasium and made preparations for the night's game.

Lucas knew, then, he had better do something about it.

I need to see you
One last time
I need to kiss you
One last goodbye

I need to tell you:
Be happy, baby
Be happy, always
Even if I'm never with you

~ Excerpt from 'Never with You'
Lyrics and music by Tara Galvez
Fragments of Us, Esta Melodia Records

CHAPTER 9

THE HEART

Tara

I T WAS HIS SMILE THAT DID IT.

The last thing her emotional state needed was a public appearance, not to mention a live performance, but one smile from Lucas Delgado was all it took for her to say yes. As she sat with his mother at the passenger seat of the pickup truck, a mix of emotions swirled within her—lingering surprise, flattery, excitement, and, above it all, apprehension.

As the walls of the high school's covered court came into view, Mercy touched her shoulder, her voice and gaze displaying equal parts motherly pride and concern. "Just one song, Tara. You'll make everyone feel very special and loved."

She swallowed and nodded, knowing the older woman was right. A song was nothing in the grand scheme of things, compared to the way the community had embraced and cherished her family for generations.

It was nearly sunset when they descended the truck and made their way into the gymnasium. Luis met them at the main entrance and relieved Tara of her guitar, guiding them through a sea of excited faces. The energy and noise was high, the sound system blaring with dance music; hundreds of students and adults were clustered on the concrete bleachers, talking excitedly.

The village's elected captain, David, a retired schoolteacher who had been friends with her grandfather, came up to them as she and Lucas' parents found their seats near the stage. Their reserved chairs, positioned in an enclosed area guarded by two burly young men, offered an unobstructed view of the basketball court.

"Thank you for agreeing to do this, Miss Tara," said David, shaking her hand enthusiastically, a proud smile on his face. "You have no idea how much this means to all of us."

"It's Mr. and Mrs. Delgado who convinced me," she replied, returning his enthusiasm with a smile of her own. "It's all them."

As they settled into their seats and watched the players take the court, Tara couldn't shake the edginess that settled in her chest, especially when Lucas jogged in their direction and gave them a jaunty thumbs-up before joining his teammates on the junior high bench.

Following a short welcome from the high school principal, the night's game was officially underway. When Lucas' name was announced, the crowd cheered wildly as he took his place against the center of the senior high school team for the jump ball.

Although she knew people in the gymnasium were merely expressing their adoration for Lucas, the noise only served to heighten her own anxiety. She fiddled with the soft material of her dress, trying to pace her breathing as she watched the players pass the ball around, ending with a boy from the junior high team making a flawless three-point shot.

As the final seconds of the first half ticked away, with Lucas' team in the lead, Tara took a deep breath, gathering her courage. As if sensing her apprehension, Mercy leaned over and put an arm around her shoulders.

"You'll be amazing, dear," she said reassuringly, giving her an affectionate squeeze. "I can't wait to hear you sing that beautiful song of yours."

As the final whistle for the game's first half sounded and the players moved to their benches, the packed building buzzed with conversation and curiosity as the event announcer made his way to the middle of the court.

"Ready, Tara?" Luis got to his feet, her guitar in one hand, while he held out his hand to help her up. The look on his face mirrored the pride she saw on Mercy's earlier. She knew she could never, ever let them down by chickening out.

She swallowed hard as she took the proffered hand and stood up. "I think so."

Mercy got to her feet, too, and gave her a quick hug. The wordless gesture was all the strength and reassurance Tara needed to get her feet to move and follow Luis up a few concrete steps to the wings of the stage.

"All the best, dear," he said, handing over her guitar. "Thank you again for doing this."

She nodded wordlessly before he left her on her own. She focused her attention on double-checking the tuning of her guitar, adjusting the tightness of the strings just so. A few feet before her, in the middle of the stage, a spotlight shone on a simple wooden stool set up behind two microphones.

The announcer cleared his throat before his energetic voice filled the court. "Our halftime show tonight is a very rare gift to us all. Our guest is a source of national pride, but she will always be a daughter of the province of Antique. Ladies and gentlemen, it is my honor to present the lady of Galvez Farms, the international music superstar, Miss Tara!"

Tara took a deep breath and stepped onto the stage, waving to the crowd as a deafening roar filled the gymnasium. She could barely see anything with the bright lights in her eyes, but she could make out that everyone was on their feet, clapping and cheering.

She arranged her face into a smile as she sat down on the stool, her fingers shaking slightly as she positioned them over the strings of her guitar. "Good evening. It's a pleasure to be here with you. Thanks to Sir David, Sir Luis, and all the school and village officials for inviting me."

As she strummed the first few notes of 'Never with You,'

the crowd stirred. A hush fell upon them as they recognized the melody; then, as if an invisible conductor had given the signal, they erupted into deafening applause that drowned out her music.

"Tara! Tara, we love you!" a voice cried out, and soon the entire gym was swaying to the rhythm of her ballad, singing along with her.

The lights of the court went out, leaving only the stage illuminated. Cellphone torches and lighters came to life as people raised them high in the air, waving to the slow beat. As with every performance, she willed her mind to be still, giving in to the raw emotion that filled her heart every time she strummed a chord and sang a verse.

But, for the first time, this performance was different.

He was here, in the same building with her.

The only person whose smile and eyes had never really left her, even after so much time and distance between them. The very subject of her melodies, now living and breathing in her life, wrenched from what only used to be a dream.

As she sang, she thought of his determination on the court, his kindness off it, his artist's soul that resonated so deeply with her own. Could he see past the mask of her self-sufficient solitude, to the fragile heart that lay beneath?

A heart that had only ever been his, since she was eighteen years old.

As if by sheer magic, her gaze drifted to stage left and there he was.

Lucas stood in the wings, half in shadow. From what she

could see, he was watching her intently, his dark eyes shining with unabashed admiration and something more.

Something that caused her breath to catch and her pulse to race.

Suddenly, he stepped onto the stage, moving toward her with purposeful strides. As he approached, he held out a bouquet of bright red roses, an equally bright and affectionate smile on his handsome face. Upon reaching her side, he dropped to one knee before her. The gesture was so unexpected, the look in his eyes so tender and genuine, that she felt a lump form in her throat, even as she kept singing.

"Kiss! Kiss! Kiss!" the crowd began to chant, their voices rising in a fevered crescendo. The heat and urgency of their excitement mingled with the weight of her own feelings—overwhelming, undeniable, almost irresistible.

"Lucas," she whispered, her guitar slipping from her grasp as she stared down at him. "I…"

But before she could finish, the pressure became too much to bear. With a choked sob, she jumped to her feet and fled the spotlight, leaving her song and her heart behind.

CHAPTER 10

THE SONG

Lucas

THE BEAUTIFUL BOUQUET SLID FROM HIS HANDS. THE girls of the high school student council had giggled and worked so hard when they put it together earlier, knowing it was meant for a 'very special lady.' Now, their arrangement landed haphazardly on the stage, scattering petals and ribbons like a tragic foreshadowing.

Lucas knelt frozen, his heart pounding erratically as he watched Tara's back retreat into the shadows of the darkened gymnasium. As her silhouette vanished beyond the wings, he lurched to his feet, his body protesting with sharp jolts of pain through his abused knee and strained lower back.

Around him, the crowd that had been pulsating with excitement now held its breath, their collective anticipation turning into a heavy curtain of unease. The raucous cheers for a kiss hushed into worried whispers.

He made his way down the steps and pushed through the mass of people that had gathered at the bottom of the stage, their faces blurred smudges on his periphery. His vision tunneled, fixated on the trail of Tara's hurried footsteps. He swallowed hard as he caught a glimpse of flowy white fabric disappearing into a side entrance.

God, she looked so beautiful in that dress.

"Lucas!" His mother's unmistakable voice cut through his fog of bewilderment, sharp and commanding.

The sight of his parents stood out from the chaos. Mercy was beside him in an instant, thrusting Tara's canvas bag into his outstretched hands. Luis followed suit, the familiar strap of Lucas' own sports bag wrapping around his fingers like a lifeline.

The words left his throat, hoarse and desperate. "I don't know what happened, Pa. She just ran…"

"She couldn't have gone far. Tara came in with your mother, so she'd be on foot." The quick, rational mind of his father was always a grounding force.

"Go after her." His mother's directive was laced with an intensity that brooked no argument, but her face began to crumble with worry and guilt. "She's fragile right now. I saw it, Luis. We could have prevented this…"

"Make sure she's okay, Lucas." Luis' voice was calm as

he wrapped a consoling arm around Mercy's shoulders. His eyes behind the glasses spoke differently, prompting for urgency. "We'll take care of things here."

Lucas nodded wordlessly before he took off in Tara's direction, slipping into the shadows and out through the side entrance. The night air was humid on his skin as he emerged into the inky, almost eerie, stillness that had settled outside the building.

"Sir Lucas!" Fred, followed closely by Marife, ran up to him, their faces bearing identical expressions of worry. "We tried to stop her, offered to take her home…"

"She told us to leave her alone," exclaimed Marife, tears welling up in her eyes. "I've never seen her so upset."

"Where did she go?" Lucas tried to keep his voice steady as his eyes swept the road, trying to orient himself in the sparse moonlight. North led to the farm, south down the mountain and into town.

"I think she's going back to the farm," Fred said quietly, gesturing to the northbound path. "Ever since she was a little girl, she always comes home to her family here…to us."

Marife's tears now flowed freely as she grabbed his hand almost painfully. "Miss Tara's got a heart made for the world to love but not to break. When her grandparents left us, she took it very hard. We thought she'd never smile again…until you came, Sir Lucas. Please bring her home."

"I…" His voice trailed off, his words quashed by the gravity of his own guilt. How badly he had put his own expectations on Tara. How stupidly he had thrown her to the public eye.

How desperately he'd wanted the world to see how much he loved her, in hopes she would see it, too.

"I'll make sure she gets home," Lucas finished lamely.

The foreman extended a small rectangular device to him. "This is for the farm gates. I'm not sure if Miss Tara brought hers. She never uses it."

"Thank you." He pocketed the remote and, with a nod to the couple, he turned and ran swiftly down the gravel lot to where the SUV was parked. His hands trembled as he rummaged through his sports bag for the keys, relief coursing through him as his fingers closed around the cold metal.

Lucas climbed onto the driver's seat, tossing his bag and Tara's to the space below the passenger dashboard. The vehicle roared to life beneath his hands, its headlights slicing through the darkness as he accelerated away.

"Come on, come on," he muttered as he drove, perspiration trickling down his temples, his heart pounding against his ribcage. His red and black jersey, a replica of his team uniform redone with logos of the local high school, was now drenched in cold sweat.

And then he saw her.

His heart leaped into his throat as he spotted Tara's white-clad silhouette several hundred meters from the gymnasium. She cut a desolate figure on the dark stretch of road, scurrying away like a wounded animal.

She flinched at the sudden intrusion of the car's harsh

lights, her shadow splintering across the road like broken wings. His stomach lurched as she turned to him, eyes wide with the kind of surprise that edged on fear.

Lucas brought the car to a shuddering halt a dozen meters ahead, blocking the path. He was out in an instant, approaching her with measured steps.

"Hey, it's okay," he said, his voice a cautious whisper, holding out his hands. "It's just me."

She recoiled with the raw instinct of someone desperately cornered, wrapping her arms around herself, her slender body still racked with sobs. "Leave me alone."

"Please." The word hung heavy between them, suspended in the tension of the moment. "Let's get you home. You need to rest."

She stepped back, retreating further into the cover of night. The vulnerability and exhaustion in the delicate lines of her face broke his heart.

"I'm not going to hurt you, Tara. I'm just here to drive you home. Please, get in the car."

She trembled as she shook her head, midnight black hair cascading over white-clad shoulders. She'd never looked more like an angel.

"I can't…" Her voice was a murmur almost lost to the breeze. "I shouldn't have come tonight. I've let everyone down. I'm so sorry."

"Hey, hey, no." He found himself stepping forward, reaching out but not touching. One wrong move and their fragile exchange would be shattered. "You didn't let anyone down. This… this is on me. I wanted—no, I needed people to see what I feel for you."

He watched the soft moonbeams dance upon her tear-streaked cheeks as she stared at him in shock. He could see himself reflected in her own gaze—a mirror of unspoken pain, carefully guarded secrets, and a life wrapped in yearning.

"What you feel for me?" she echoed, the words fading into a look of disbelief on her face.

"What I feel doesn't matter if it's making you like this." He shook his head, overcome by an overwhelming tide of guilt as he tried to make sense of his own actions. "I'm so sorry. I should have given you space, not crossed your boundaries. This isn't a game, after all. It's you…and you mean more to me than any game—or anything, or anyone."

His own defenses, the barriers he'd erected to shield his career, his heart, his very soul from the inevitable injuries of life and love, crumbled beneath the weight of his own words.

"I wish I could be brave as you are." Her voice, usually so clear when wrapped around the notes of her songs, was now thin and shaky. "I'm afraid of the whole fucking world, do you know that? I'm afraid of opening up and being told I'm not enough, of being rejected and told my songs are no longer worth listening to."

"Don't say that—" he protested, but she wasn't listening.

Tara continued, her voice faraway as if she was trying to capture a poignant, distant memory. "I've traveled so far and wide, all over the world. I was fine always on my own for so many years. I don't need to open up, right? I have my music. It's everything to me, Lucas. It's all I have."

Her words stirred something within him, a protective instinct mingling with profound reverence for her honesty that allowed him a glimpse into her heart. This woman before him was not just an artist; she was every note of every song she'd ever written.

He closed the distance between them, his arms encircling her as gently as he could. He was ready for her to push him away, ready for her to put up yet another wall between them. Ready for her to reject everything he was willing to give.

Lucas Delgado had gone past caring whether or not he got hurt. This time, it would be worth it.

"No, you have people here who love you," he murmured into her hair. "You have the farm. And you've got me, too. You'll always have me."

He could feel the tension in her body, an instinctive resistance heartbreakingly familiar to him. But slowly, she softened, her defenses faltering in his embrace.

She didn't say anything. Instead, she melted against him, burying her face in his shirt, her shoulders still heaving from residual sobs. He'd held her so many times before, but it was only tonight he realized just how small and fragile she really was.

"Let me get you home," he said softly. "Let me take care of you. Just for tonight."

She nodded, barely, but it was enough for him. He lifted

her carefully and settled her onto the front seat. As he fastened the seatbelt around her, the soft click resonated like a lock falling into place around his own heart.

In that moment, the truth became undeniable.

He loved Tara Galvez. He always had.

His fingers lingered near her face, the urge to caress her skin almost overpowering, but he hesitated, respecting the trust she was tentatively offering him. Instead, he placed her canvas bag on her lap.

She glanced around uncertainly. "My guitar…"

"My parents will take care of it. I'll get it back for you in the morning. Don't worry, okay?"

She nodded, clutching her bag to her chest.

The road back to the farm stretched out before them, a still, empty path lined with gently swaying palm trees. In the moonlight, their shadows almost looked like the audience back at the gymnasium, moving as one to the beat of her music.

And he'd promptly ruined it.

Trying to ignore another wave of guilt that made his chest constrict, he focused on using the loaned remote to open the heavy wooden gates of Galvez Farms.

"Is that Fred's?"

"Yeah. He wasn't sure if you had yours. My parents, Fred and Marife…they all told me to bring you home."

"They didn't have to worry," she commented quietly, her gaze trained on the darkness outside her window. "I'll always be safe in this village."

We thought she'd never smile again…until you came, Sir Lucas. Please bring her home.

Marife's words. A wealth of insight into the soul of the woman next to him, captured in such a short statement.

Home. It was a word that was slowly becoming synonymous with Tara's presence in his life.

"Doesn't stop us from caring," he replied gently, as he navigated the bends of the dirt road that snaked towards the main villa.

He parked as close to the house as possible. The engine's hum faded, leaving only the sound of their breathing to fill the quiet void between them.

"Do you know why I'm here, Lucas?" Her unexpected question cut through the silence like a knife.

He couldn't even think of a reply that didn't make him sound ignorant or insensitive. He chose an honest answer instead. "I don't know…Fred and Marife said you always came home."

"Did they? I suppose they're right, in their own way. This is my home…I chose it. When I'm home I'm not supposed to doubt myself. I shouldn't be afraid. But you know what? I'm scared as fuck."

"Tara, I—"

She cut him off—or she probably didn't even hear him speak. "I've been putting off my third album. I've been having nightmares that I don't have the material or talent anymore to keep going. I'm afraid that if and when I manage to get it done, I'll be heavily criticized. I came home to escape those doubts, Lucas, but I couldn't run from my own head. Tonight made that very clear."

He cast a sidelong glance at her; she was staring straight ahead, at a faint path of moonbeams past the windshield, her beautiful face drawn and almost deathly pale. The sight made his throat constrict painfully. What he thought would be a romantic gesture had caused a shitstorm he'd probably never be able to fix.

"When people's hearts are on you and your success, you can't afford to let them down. That's what's killing me. I can't even talk to my parents or Jasmine about it because I know they'll worry and most likely send me off for help. I don't want that—I just want to be with my music. But tonight, with all those people, with you in front of me…everything just fell apart." Tara sighed deeply, then cleared her throat. "Anyway, it's a miracle I'm back here in one piece. I've got you to thank for that."

He heard the finality in her tone, knew he couldn't push her any further. Instead, he nodded and undid his seatbelt to get out of the car. He was about to reach for the door handle when something stopped him—the need to know he was still allowed in her life.

"I didn't mean to put you through all this, Tara. I'm so sorry. I'll do anything to make it up to you."

She didn't respond at first. Instead, she undid her own seatbelt and slid forward on the front seat, her hands settling on the dashboard before she turned to look in his direction.

In the faint moonlight, her eyes looked like deep pools of gold.

When she finally spoke, the words sounded muted. "Why did you do that at the game, Lucas? The flowers, the kneeling, the spotlight…If a showbiz performance was what you wanted, you should have told me from the get-go. I've been in the business for a long time."

He shook his head. "That wasn't a performance."

"Then what was it?" she pressed in a stronger voice, her brows furrowing. "Some kind of prank? I thought we were… friends. Why put up a show like that at my expense?"

"That wasn't a show," he countered, knowing at the back of his mind that whatever followed, he had better be prepared for the consequences. "I meant everything I did—and everything I said. From the day I first got to this place and saw you again, I knew I couldn't stay away. I wanted to be with you, Tara. I wanted to kiss you and hold you and protect you… and I needed you and the whole world to know."

He stopped, head spinning from adrenaline. Then he saw it: a flicker of something raw and unguarded in her eyes as she regarded him, stupefied.

To his utter surprise, her emotions broke free, stealing what little breath he had left away.

With a strangled cry, Tara threw herself at him fiercely, mounting him right there on the driver's seat. His hands instinctively rose to meet her as she kissed him—a kiss without any remaining facade of restraint.

He responded with equal fervor, the sweet taste of her

lips igniting the fire of passion that had long since smoldered within him. The world outside the confines of the car ceased to exist; there was only her and her touch and her heady vanilla scent, the weight of her damp body on his lap a million times better than any fevered dream.

The kiss was hungry and desperate, quashing any hesitation he had left at his ragged, sweat-soaked state. Her fingers slipped beneath his jersey, tracing the contours of his abdomen. He responded enthusiastically by lifting the hem of her white dress, the fabric gliding against his hands as he cupped the softness of her skin protected only by the flimsy barrier of her underwear. Eager to taste her, he pushed his tongue into her mouth. She moaned in response, her hands tugging at his hair as she ground against him, a silent confession of her need.

He slid her upward, pressing his lips to the swell of her breasts through the thin fabric of her dress. His breath ghosted over the bare skin of her neckline, eliciting a shiver that he felt reverberate through his own body.

She writhed above him, her movements stirring his desire into an almost desperate hunger for more of her, all of her. Reaching around, his fingers found the heat of her, slick and welcoming. He stroked her then, fingers sliding in and out, watching her face contort with pleasure, listening to her moans fill the car—a melody sweeter than any song she had ever sung.

His breath caught when she reached down and tugged at his shorts. He lifted his hips and, together, they both managed to pull it down along with his briefs, releasing his throbbing arousal. He lost no time in pressing his maddening hardness against the dampness of her panties, his hands cupping the sides of her hips, asking for permission.

"Yes," she groaned, "always yes."

A muffled gasp escaped her lips when, in one determined movement, he pushed the tiny piece of fabric down, baring her just enough to join his body with hers.

"*Fuck,* Tara." The sensation of being inside her was so, so good. She was warm and wet and welcoming, everything he had imagined her to feel but amplified a thousandfold. "What are you doing to me?"

She didn't answer but clung to him tighter, their foreheads pressing together, remnants of her tears trickling onto his skin. She wound her arms around his neck as her hips began to move in slow circles. The friction caused jolts of electricity to course through his body, making him lose all sense except the feel of her in his arms.

"Lucas… Lucas…" she sang against his lips, fingers tracing patterns on the skin behind his ears, every motion of her lithe body a note that pushed him deeper and deeper into abandon.

He thrust back into her, his cock enveloped by the white-hot heat of her pussy, and he was lost in the sensation, drowning in the heady scent of her skin and their shared passion. He buried his face in her neck as they moved together in a pounding, increasingly wild rhythm that she controlled.

"God, you're perfect," he whispered into her ear, nipping

at the soft skin now beaded with sweat. "Everything I've always wanted."

Tara responded by rotating her hips with increased urgency, throwing her head back uninhibitedly as her moans grew louder. His mouth found her nipples through the fabric of her dress, sucking each in turn to add to her pleasure, knowing she was close to the brink.

"Lucas," she gasped, and it was not just his name; it was a plea, an affirmation, a surrender. Her body tensed in the most intimate of ways, and then her mouth opened in a silent, shuddering scream.

He felt the surge building within him as her body gyrated and shook in the throes of her release, the pressure and pleasure intermingling within him until he could no longer distinguish where one ended and the other began.

He followed her then, his own climax tearing through him, declared triumphantly to the quiet night by a hoarse shout he could no longer contain.

A simple truth he could no longer hide.

"I love you, Tara. I love you."

I feel my body steaming towards you
I burn in flames of passion
Until I am nothing more
Than trembling desire

I feel my soul steaming towards you
I surrender all of me
Until I am nothing more
Than your wasted possession

~ Excerpt from 'Nothing'
Lyrics and music by Tara Galvez
I Remember You, Esta Melodia Records

CHAPTER 11

THE SECRET

Tara

SHE WAS HIS NOW. IT HAS ALWAYS BEEN SO.

She didn't know how long they clung to each other, still intimately entwined on the driver's seat as his confession hung in the air. His wavy hair was damp against her skin, tickling her cheeks as she breathed against him, momentarily spent. He smelled of sweat and citrus, his breath hot on her collarbone.

He was the first to move, slowly, almost reluctantly. He lifted his head, gaze meeting hers in the dim light as his hands caressed her hair, smoothing errant locks away from her face. "I've always loved you, you know."

Love.

One word, one thing she'd held on to, all these years. Her quiet sort of madness.

She had pined for this man half her life, watched and adored him from afar, robbed herself of the chance to experience something else with someone other than this tall, wavy-haired creature, whose piercing eyes had never stopped haunting her.

So much time, now wrapped up in this moment with him in her arms, Lucas saying the words she'd never expected to hear him utter outside of her dreams.

She didn't answer, allowing herself to go limp in his embrace as he carefully lifted her from his lap and settled her back onto the front seat. As they awkwardly fixed their clothes, the world around her came into soft focus, the windows and windshield of the car still fogged by their passion

He didn't demand an answer. Instead, Lucas caressed her cheek for a few precious, stolen seconds, before reaching for the door handle.

She caught his hand and brought it to her lips. His fingers still bore traces of her own scent as she kissed them tenderly.

"Will you stay?"

He smiled then, reminding her of the time she'd first invited him to dinner. "Of course. Let's get you inside."

With one last peck on her lips, he exited the car and opened the passenger door. He shouldered both his bag and hers, the sight making her giggle, and lifted her out of the vehicle. She pulled him close for a kiss before he set her back down. She led him by the hand, up the porch and into the house, locking the door behind them, sealing the world away.

With a deep breath, she silently made her way to a staircase in a part of the villa he'd never seen before. He followed closely, at one point pausing midway through the flight of steps to wrap his arms around her and kiss the back of her neck.

"I love you," he said softly, again.

The words exhilarated and scared her.

For the first time in her life, she led a man to her sanctuary: a large, airy bedroom nestled in the far corner of the house.

"Is this…?" Lucas broke the silence as soon as she switched on the soft lights. His eyes took in the walls decorated with framed photographs of a younger Tara with her family and childhood friends, as well as more recent images of her portraits and album covers.

"Mine."

Tara took a deep breath and slowly shed her clothes, piece by piece, until she stood completely bare under his smoldering gaze. She felt exposed, but more than anything, she wanted him to see her. Wordlessly, she backed towards the bathroom, never breaking eye contact. As soon as she arrived, trembling and flushed, she turned on the shower and stepped under the warm cascade of water.

It barely took a minute before Lucas joined her under

the spray. His lips met hers in a searing kiss, his naked body pressed tightly against hers.

Nothing had prepared her for the moment she could finally touch all of him. Her fingers traced wide shoulders and an equally broad chest, then slid down to explore a taut stomach and narrow hips. His legs were beautifully sinewy and strong and, between them, his arousal stood proud and unapologetic.

She heard him suck a breath in as her hands closed around the rock-hard length of him, tugging, caressing, claiming.

"Can I touch you, too?" he asked breathlessly between kisses. "All of you?"

"Yes," she murmured against his lips, her heart hammering in her chest at the idea of being so vulnerable.

He pushed her against the bathroom wall, his arms on either side of her, holding her up. He showered her with gentle kisses and caresses; on her lips, cheeks, nose, ears, neck, and collarbone, leaving a trail of heat with his mouth and fingers.

As he touched her bare breasts for the first time, her breath caught in her throat, thinking of the well-endowed actresses and models he was so often photographed with. To her surprise, he looked up with an adoring smile on his face, and his voice was filled with wonder when he said, "They're perfect—made to fit into my hand." She felt a sense of relief and happiness wash over her as he suckled her nipples like a starving man.

He kissed his way down to her stomach, spreading her legs as he did so. He knelt before her as if worshipping at an altar, the tenderness of his actions almost making her cry.

How she loved this man. But, even in the midst of their passion, she couldn't find the words to tell him.

And he was only getting started.

He positioned one of her legs over his shoulder, his hand stroking her pussy and the thin patch of hair surrounding it, his touch tickling her in the most intimate of ways.

"You're so beautiful," he said, his lips inches away from her heat. "So fucking beautiful."

She could only watch in awe as he proceeded to place her other leg over his shoulder, supporting her against the wall with his own strength. Then his lips, tongue, and mouth dove into her, licking, circling, and sucking.

"Lucas," she gasped, grinding against his mouth, wave after wave of pleasure rippling through her.

He responded by using his tongue to trace the length of her slit, causing her to squirm and squeal, before he looked up into her eyes. "Let go, love. I've got you."

His mouth was back on her, bringing her to a slow, delicious, soul-rending climax that made her soar to a peak she'd never reached before. She didn't know how long she stayed there, eyes tightly shut, breathless and finally uncaring. She was only aware that his name lingered on her lips as aftershocks of her orgasm tore through her body.

When she finally opened her eyes, he was standing

before her, supporting her limp form with a smile on his lips. Lucas looked tall and beautiful under the splashing water, his desire undeniable in his eyes and the rock-hard flesh between his muscled thighs.

"Kiss me," she commanded softly, putting her arms around his waist.

He obeyed without hesitation. As their lips met, she tasted herself on him, bringing forth a fresh wave of hunger. She knew she wanted to feel him inside her again.

"Let's finish what we started in the garden, Lucas."

This time, he paused, pulling back slightly to look into her eyes. "Are you sure? You just…you know."

"Yes. Always yes." Echoing what she'd said in the car earlier, she jumped into his arms, knowing he would catch her.

He eased her back against the cool tiles once more, her legs wrapped around his hips as he entered her for the second time that night. He suckled her breasts while he pumped into her, measured and deliberate at first, until his pace increased in urgency and passion. He growled against her skin, his teeth grazing and marking her flesh, until he shook and cursed as he climaxed.

Though dazed and trembling, Lucas didn't leave her wanting. He used one hand to reach between their bodies, using nimble fingers and his large, throbbing length to coax her body towards another shattering release.

Tara collapsed into his arms, unable to support her own weight from the sheer force of the pleasure he'd given her. To her surprise, he lowered her to her feet, one arm supporting her, his free hand lathering liquid soap all over her hair and heated flesh. He rinsed and kissed her in turn, then wrapped her in a towel and carried her to the bed.

"I'll be back, love." She heard the words in a dreamy haze, felt the softness of her own sheets against her skin. She reached out to stroke his damp hair, lovingly, trying to muster a reassuring smile for his benefit. She watched him turn off the lights in the bedroom and make his way back to the shower.

Kind, considerate, gentle, passionate Lucas.

A tear escaped her eye. If only she was brave enough to tell him he'd been the muse behind all her songs. If only she could admit that unspoken love had fueled her music for years. Instead, she let the steady sound of running water lull her to a peaceful slumber.

She didn't know how long she'd been asleep, but she slowly stirred to wakefulness with an overwhelming feeling of warmth enveloping her. At first, she thought it was merely her blankets, but as she shifted slightly, she became aware of the strong arm wrapped securely around her, holding her close against a bare chest.

The moonlight streaming through the curtains fell on Lucas' sleeping form, his features chiseled and unbearably beautiful in the thin, silvery light. Surely, this wasn't real. The sight of him lying beside her was, as always, just another fleeting dream.

With tentative fingers, she reached out and traced the

curve of his cheek. As her touch grazed his skin, his eyes fluttered open in drowsy surprise. He murmured words of love, his voice thick with sleep, before closing his lids once more.

"Lucas," she whispered, feeling a surge of courage well up inside her as she leaned in and pressed her lips to his.

His arms tightened around her, his hands weaving through her hair and gliding over her back and buttocks. Even in his half-asleep state, he responded to her kiss with matching fervor.

She climbed atop him and deepened the kiss, rubbing her naked body against his, feeling him come to life underneath her. He eagerly explored her body with his hands, finding her breasts and then daring to reach between her thighs.

"Steady on, big boy." She playfully pushed his hands away. "Let me."

"Yes, ma'am." He chuckled and held himself still, allowing her to take control.

She slid down his body, leaving a trail of delicate kisses along his chest and abdomen. Her lips found his nipples, biting them gently before continuing their journey downward. As she reached Lucas's powerful thighs, her hands found the waistband of his boxers. With a determined tug, she pulled down the shorts, revealing his arousal standing at attention.

"Fuck, Tara." His voice was thick with desire as his

hands slid into her hair, his fingers warm and possessive at the nape of her neck.

She closed her fingers around his cock, keeping her grip firm yet gentle as she began stroking him rhythmically. Her lips and tongue danced across his balls, raining kisses, licks, nips, and suckles that had his hips bucking. He groaned and cursed loudly, praises falling from his lips.

"Keep going, love," he urged her, in a voice strained with the effort of holding back.

She looked up, only to see his eyes melting into dark pools of passion. She finally took him into her mouth, knowing he was teetering on the brink.

She switched her focus, her hands now massaging his balls while her lips enveloped his cock. She tugged and sucked gently, increasing her pace every few seconds. His moans grew as he neared breaking point; his hands tightened in her hair, too, but she didn't stop.

Then he broke, hips shooting into the air as he climaxed, shouting with abandon, "Tara, Tara, fuck, I love you." His voice rang throughout the house as his release filled her mouth, and she swallowed it all.

She crawled up next to him and lay quietly as she waited for him to recover, his chest heaving as he struggled to catch his breath. She watched as his eyes slowly began to focus, finally settling on her face inches away.

With a tender smile, he opened his arms. "Love."

She hesitated for a brief moment, but she couldn't resist the longing in his gaze. She snuggled into his embrace, welcoming the warmth of his arms around her. He leaned down to kiss her hair and forehead as she listened to his heartbeat, marveling as its pace slowed down to sync with hers.

"Do you know why I'm here? In this village?"

The question, uttered in a rumbling whisper known only to lovers, came completely out of the blue, a twisted echo of her earlier confession.

"Lucas…I…I don't know. You said you wanted to take a break from the city, right?"

He must have sensed her growing unease, for he tightened his hold on her, his voice losing none of its soft timbre. "I came here to get away—away from Manila and my team, away from everyone's scrutiny. I figured this was the best place to clear my head and think things through."

She couldn't quite get the point he was trying to make, but she understood his meaning. She was here for the exact same reason. "Because…?"

"My career might be ending soon." The words escaped his lips in a rush. "Much sooner than most people believe it would."

Confusion coursed through her, followed closely by a sense of disbelief. He could be joking, but it was something so far out of character for a man like him.

"Why?" It was the only question, the only word that could help her make sense of this.

He sighed. "I've been injured. I've been hurt, a whole lot. Pulled back muscles that won't completely heal, broken kneecaps patched up, ribs that have taken so much damage they might snap. After our first Philippine Cup championship two years ago, the other teams made it their main goal to put me out of commission. They always assigned larger, rougher players against me just to cause more damage. It would be funny if it didn't hurt like fuck."

"But…you're still so strong," she fumbled, shaking her head. "Just as strong as when you first started playing in the league. Maybe even stronger."

"Maybe I'm good at putting up a show," he offered gently. "So good, no one could see I was falling apart right in front of them."

"No," she muttered against his chest, hearing echoes of her own secrets in his confessions. "No."

"I'm old, love," he continued wryly, "and broken. But you…you make me whole again. That's why I was so grateful when I saw you. Seeing you here made me feel alive and hopeful. Maybe I had another chance, you know? Maybe it wasn't the end for me."

Tara could feel her heart breaking as he spoke of the pain and vulnerability that had been hidden beneath his confident façade.

"Who else knows about this?" she asked tentatively. "Surely someone else does…"

"Yeah, my manager, coach, and trainer all know. They've done an excellent job at hiding it from the public and even my teammates, but it's only a matter of time before the signs become visible. Even the team owner is in on the secret. I wanted to drop my contract and suffer the penalties. He refused to let me go, though. These people still believe in me, for some reason."

"And your family?"

"I…They can't know, Tara. Especially my parents."

"I believe in you. I'll never stop believing in you." She pressed her lips against his cheek, nuzzling the thin stubble along his jawline. "Whatever you tell me will stay between us."

His admission struck so painfully close to her own fears. The crushing weight of expectations, the even heavier burden of keeping one's struggles hidden from those closest to them. She never realized two completely different lives on the surface could be so alike underneath, once the glitter of fame was stripped off.

Lucas turned his face to hers, capturing her lips in a kiss. "But you…I wanted to tell you the truth, from the very start. I don't want secrets between us."

She nodded in silent agreement and brought her arms up, encircling his neck, deepening the kiss.

He seemed to be done speaking, as he rolled her onto her back. He covered her body with his, his tongue making its sweet way into her mouth. His fingers traced a heated path along her collarbone, his touch making her squirm for more. Her breath hitched as he moved lower, caressing her breasts. His hand was replaced by his mouth, leaving a trail of kisses down her stomach.

He didn't have to ask; Tara opened her legs for him,

just as she opened her heart to his love and trust that very moment.

Lucas gave a groan of approval, his hands warm on her thighs as his mouth found her core, lapping up her juices greedily with his tongue, his lips sucking her nub until her legs were in the air, until she was gasping his name in abandon.

It was her turn to hold her arms open for him. He went into her embrace, their lips meeting in a fierce kiss that tasted of her and him.

"Never let go, love," Lucas murmured into her ear, as he positioned himself between her legs.

"Never."

Then he was inside her, their bodies moving together in languid strokes. Her hips rose to meet his steady thrusts; as pleasure built within her, she brought her legs higher, wider, wanting him to take all of her.

"Yes, my love, yes," he encouraged, his voice thick and rough with passion.

She clung to him, her nails raking down his back as they kissed fervently, his strokes intensifying as her own pleasure built right along with his urgency. And then, just as she thought she couldn't bear it any longer, her climax crashed over her, an irresistible torrent of sensation and emotion.

"Lucas," she gasped into his neck as he pounded into her with a desire bordering on desperate.

She felt him tense up and fill her, heard him groan her

name into the night, tasted his sweat on her lips as he kissed her once more before his head crashed onto her chest.

As she put her arms around him and stroked his hair, listening to him breathe against her own trembling body, she knew with all her heart that she now belonged to him in a way that could never be undone.

CHAPTER 12

THE DREAM

H E AWOKE TO A WARM GLOW, BEFORE HIS EYES AND inside his heart.

Soft light filtered through the curtains of an unfamiliar room, the rays of sunshine almost golden. Lucas found himself holding Tara flush against his own body as she slept soundly, her chest rising and falling gently with each breath.

This was her bedroom.

He couldn't see a clock anywhere. He was certain his cellphone was buried somewhere in his bag, which he'd haphazardly dropped in a corner of the room the night before. As she stirred in his arms, he pulled her closer, feeling a wave of arousal wash over him when he realized they were both still naked.

He buried his face in the nape of her neck, inhaling the intoxicating scent of her hair. He felt her body shift against his, pressing her backside against his hips, causing his hardness to grow further. Unable to resist any longer, he began to pepper her neck, hair, and shoulders with tender kisses. "I love you so much, Tara."

"Lucas," she responded sleepily, snuggling deeper into his embrace. "You feel so good…so warm. Please don't stop."

"I won't," he promised, and began to kiss and nip at her upper back in earnest, rubbing his throbbing cock against her buttocks.

She moaned in response, reaching up to pull at his hair as she ground back against him. "I never knew it could feel like this."

"Neither did I, love. But we're together now…and this is only the beginning."

"Oh, yes," she sighed, as his tongue found the sensitive skin at the back of her neck. "Yes, we've only just begun, haven't we?"

He chuckled in satisfaction at the unspoken challenge in her words. He reached for her breasts, cupping and squeezing, fingers flicking over her nipples. He could wake up to this every day.

"Play a song for me?" he whispered into her ear as he reached for her hand and guided it between her legs. "Play this song only for me, love."

"Lucas, I…" She flushed, turning her face away.

"You're so ready," he encouraged, tracing the heat of her with a finger, eliciting a small yelp that made him laugh lightly. "So wet. I would eat you, but let's do it your way first." He nudged his cock against her back entrance, almost entering her. "Please?"

"Oh, Lucas…" She hesitated for a moment, but under the guidance of his hand, her fingers took a life of their own.

"Yes," he murmured in satisfaction, watching her hips begin to move under her own touch. He lifted himself up by the elbow to get a better view, entranced. "Keep going, love."

Bathed by sunlight trickling into her room, Tara's naked form was even more breathtaking than last night. Her black hair, spread on the pillow like wings, stood out in stark contrast to the creamy-white color of her skin. She had the most perfectly round and perky breasts, perched on a flawless torso that had a narrow waist and softly curved hips. Her face was angelic, but her body was irresistibly tempting—and, now, here she was before him, his name dripping from her lips while she rubbed herself.

Her moans reached a crescendo, her knees bending and spreading to give way to the pleasure she was trying to reach. He watched in wonder as her palm stroked in circles, fingers dipping in and out, hips bucking to the tune of a song only the two of them could hear.

"Fuck, love, you're so beautiful." Unable to resist, he bent down and captured her lips, tongue tangling with hers, groaning when he saw her other hand pinch her own nipples.

"I'm coming, Lucas," she gasped against his mouth, breasts bouncing against his chest, "I'm so close."

"I'm right here, right here." He was a team player, after all, so he joined in the last few beats of her performance. He reached for her wrists and gently positioned her palms over her breasts. "Go high, and I'll finish low."

He lowered his head between her legs, draping her knees over his shoulders, and dove right into the fray. He licked and suckled at the moist path left by her hand as she continued caressing her own nipples, writhing under their combined ministrations. Her juices spilled over his tongue and, in an explosive thrust of her hips and a scream of his name, she came on his lips.

He slid up to the pillows and took her in his arms, carrying on with his soft kisses to her hair, now damp and askew. She curled into his chest, mewling softly as her body shook from the echoes of her climax.

"I'm right here," he repeated, his lips brushing her temple, making their way down to the curve of her jawline. "I've got you."

"Lucas…Lucas…" she moaned into the crook of his neck as her arms went around him, her breasts melding perfectly to the skin of his torso as if they'd always belonged there.

The intimacy of the moment was not lost on him as he tightened his embrace, nuzzling her hair. But his body was a ravenous beast in her presence; just as she slid her leg to settle between his knees, his rock-hard cock reared its head in hunger.

"Is that…?" Her eyes fluttered open, thick lashes sweeping shadows around her face.

Fuck.

It was her gaze that undid him, as he felt his arousal respond by poking at her thigh.

"Yeah…he's a little excited. I'm sorry. It's just that you're so beautiful and he can't help himself."

A pure, tinkling laugh signaled her complete understanding. Instead of saying something, Tara reached up to his hair and tugged his head down to hers. She kissed him full on the mouth, passionately and breathlessly, leaving no room for doubt.

Lucas eagerly accepted her unspoken consent, kissing her back as his hands slid down to cup her backside. He dipped a finger into her, circling his large palms over the soft cheeks of flesh. "Can he come in this way, love? I think he really wants to, if that's okay."

A blush crept up Tara's cheeks as she nodded, giggling. "Sure."

He got up and guided her into position, her body poised on all fours at the edge of the bed. He leaned in to plant a kiss at the back of her neck as he reached over to stroke her wetness, making sure she was ready.

And she was.

A surge of possessive need coursed through him as he straightened, already exhilarated at the sight of her buttocks on full display. With a deep breath, he found a firm grip on her hips and entered her from behind in one swift motion.

She gasped, her body stiffening. She felt hot and unbelievably tight.

"Are you okay?"

"Yes," she answered breathily. "You feel so good….oh…"

He began to move inside her, gradually gaining intensity until his moans were loud enough for the entire farm to hear. He used one hand to hold her steady while the other roamed her body, claiming every inch of her as his own.

"Do you like this version of our song?" His fingers reached between her legs, dancing over her clit in time with the rhythm of his thrusts.

"Keep playing," she moaned, and he obeyed, taking her higher and higher.

As his own peak neared, he increased the tempo of his thrusts and his fingers, until he had completely and clearly drawn the pleasure out of his body and hers.

As they collapsed onto the bed, he held her close, his lips seeking the damp strands that clung to her forehead. She reached up, too, threading her hands through his hair, eyes closed as she panted against him.

Slowly, he eased their bodies back up towards the pillows and pulled the blanket over her. "Are you okay?"

"Never better." She opened her eyes a touch, stirring in his arms to a more comfortable position on her side. "What time is it?"

"I don't know," he admitted. "But I don't care. I've got you with me and that's all I care about."

She sighed, smiling as she settled her head on his chest. "It makes perfect sense when you put it that way. I've only ever had you in my dreams before—*this* is way better."

He cupped her chin gently, turning her face back towards him. "I was in your dreams?"

"Lucas…" Her eyes darted away from his.

"You don't have to tell me anything right now," he said quickly, unwilling to put her on the spot. He let her chin go and embraced her. "I'm sorry."

"It's okay," she murmured. "I've never done this before."

"Sorry," he said again, stroking her back and hair.

Silence fell over them, and he found his eyelids growing heavy. He wanted to give in to sleep, but he also wanted to savor every waking second of having Tara in his arms, spent and flushed from his lovemaking.

"Lucas." Her voice was barely above a whisper, barely awake. "The first time you came here…what made you say that you felt as if I was singing only to you?"

"I don't know. There was just something in your voice that always made me feel like you were right there beside me whenever I listened to your music. It felt like the words you were singing were meant only for me to hear and understand. Crazy, huh?"

Tara exhaled slowly, her hands easing up to clutch at his shoulders. When she spoke, he could barely hear the words. "You're not wrong. My songs—all of them—have been meant for you."

She could have shouted them; the shock that went through his body was enough to stun him motionless.

She took a deep breath and continued, her voice trembling. "That song last night, 'Never with You,' it was for you. I wrote it when I first heard you got picked in the pro league draft."

He felt something warm and wet splash on his chest. She was crying.

She went on talking, in that haunting melodious voice of hers. "The reason it was so hard for me to sing last night was that I never imagined I would be doing it in front of you. And you were kneeling and all before me, with flowers…so I got out of there as fast as I could."

A disbelieving rush of joy shot through his body as he absorbed the weight of her words. "You were very fast, love. I thought I was fucked for sure."

She snorted through her tears, her light sobs giving way to giggles. "Well, you did get fucked, didn't you? Several times, I might add. Maybe a few more times if you behave yourself."

He joined her laughter and pecked her soundly on the lips, wiping her tears away with his thumbs. "I promise I'll behave if you kiss me."

Her lips found his in a breathless, passionate kiss. "I'm so glad I finally had the chance to tell you…I thought I'd get over it, but even after all those songs and so many years, things haven't changed."

He felt a smile break through his face, like dawn slipping through the darkest cracks of night. He felt it warm every fiber of what made him whole.

She did. Tara Galvez made him whole.

"You know why they haven't changed? Because, through all that time, I have never stopped loving you."

It was as if
I danced with you
In the shadows
I danced with you
In the rain

I danced with you
To a beat
Only love remembers

~ Excerpt from 'Rain'
Lyrics and music by Tara Galvez
Fragments of Us, Esta Melodia Records

CHAPTER 13

THE CONFESSION

Tara

Y EARS. THEY MEASURED TIME, BUT NO ONE HAD EVER told her they would also mean endless nights, hidden fears, and desolate walls.

The years had put her in a gilded cage of success and fame, where inside her heart had begun to wither. Sometimes she wondered why it was still beating.

Now, she knew the answer.

Her heart was still beating for him, *with his*.

And now, she needed more answers.

"You have…*loved* me for that long?" Tara still fumbled over the word. Writing about love was one thing; living it was something else entirely. "I thought you never even noticed me back then. I was a nobody back in college."

"Trust me, I noticed you." The gentle, reassuring smile on Lucas' face was the stuff of grand epic romances, of love lost and found. It was a smile that touched and overwhelmed her in equal measure. "You were never nobody to me. You were always the most beautiful girl I'd ever seen, and now… you're even more stunning as a woman."

He continued, his baritone like music to her ears, his tender caresses on her hair and cheek making her own heart sing. "Ever since the time you returned my sketchbook, I've wanted nothing more than to be with you. I've followed your career, bought all your CDs, and even attended your concert once, hiding at the last row like an idiot."

"I never knew…" Their years apart had made sure of that. "Why didn't you tell me sooner? Why didn't you send me a message or ask to see me after my show?"

Lucas moved to a seated position, easing her up along with him. The look in his eyes as he took in her bare breasts was enough to make her blush.

"How could I?" His voice was filled with awe as he reached out to run his fingers through her hair. "You are a star, Tara, and you shine like no one else does. Dumb jocks like me could only stand back and love you from a distance. But your music…it was my way of keeping you close. It's been the soundtrack of my life, ever since I heard your first song." His fingers made their slow journey downward, tracing her eyes, cheeks, and lips. "What was it? Ah, 'Rain.'"

She closed her eyes and let his words and touch wash over her. She grabbed his hand, keeping it on her cheek, loving its warmth on her skin.

"I've never had a meaningful relationship with anyone," he added wryly. "Didn't matter who or what they were…no one could compare to you. I just ended up listening to you sing, night after night."

With a soft cry, she threw herself into his arms. "You idiot, you should have said something. You should have *at least* asked for your damn jacket back."

"Now that I think about that jacket…have you still got it?"

She hugged him tighter. "It's in the closet, first door on the right."

Lucas laughed as he pressed his lips to her cheek. "It's not too late for us, is it? Tell me, is there someone who would want to put me six feet under for what we've been doing since last night?"

She playfully punched him on the chest, a smile breaking through her tears as she shook her head. "There's no one else."

"There's a chance for me, then, isn't there? Would you give me a chance?"

She didn't answer. She couldn't answer.

Instead, she slid out of his arms and got to her feet. Naked, she made a beeline for the closet and retrieved his old varsity jacket from its hiding place. She slid her arms through its voluminous sleeves as she made her way back to him.

He watched her every move, still as a statue from his

perch on the bed. The desire in his eyes was unmistakable, burning brighter with each step she took closer.

"It still fits," she declared.

"It still fits," he echoed, biting his lip as he held out his arms to her. "Yeah."

"Sometimes, I still wear this," she said, crawling back towards him. "You know, when it's cold…and when I dream of you."

She felt Lucas stiffen as she straddled him, her breasts promptly pushing up to his face as she put her hands on his shoulders.

"Dream of me, love?" He caught on quickly, his arms encircling her waist.

She smiled down at him. "Sometimes, I dream of what it feels like to be held by those arms, to be touched by those hands. The usual things a girl dreams about."

"Tell me more," he urged, his lips finding their way to a taut nipple.

"My favorite dream is this." She reached for his hardness, impressed at how quickly it responded, then guided it to her slick entrance. "Nothing beats this."

She sank onto him, sheathing him inside her. She gasped at the sensation of being completely filled, of being in control of something so raw.

"Let's see if we can beat your dream." He gave her a roguish smile full of promise.

They moved together, she clinging to him as he thrust up into her with determined strokes. The world around them faded away once more, leaving only the ebb and flow of their passion, the firm grip of his hands on her hips, and the sound of his moans echoing her own.

"This is fucking better than any dream," he said through gritted teeth. "Don't stop, love."

Encouraged by his words, she rotated her hips in a wider circle, pumping herself up and down, feeling an exquisite agony intensify with every motion. His hands on her tightened, seeking control of her movements, and she could feel him trembling beneath her.

"You're right," she gasped. "This is way better."

She leaned back, allowing her own pleasure to build unchecked. Her body was a symphony ready to be mastered, as she offered her breasts and clit for him to caress, desperate for his touch on the rest of her.

"Tara…Tara…." Lucas' words were urgent as his fingers began to work their magic. The pleasure built and built until it threatened to make her lose all control.

"Oh god, Lucas…" she cried out, teetering on the very edge, already lost in sensations far better than any wild dream could give.

Before she realized what was happening, Lucas had flipped her onto her back, her legs over his shoulders as he took over, pumping into her with a hunger she'd never experienced before. The sudden shift of position caught her off guard, and her climax caught her unawares, ripping through her without quarter, leaving her breathless and utterly consumed by a giant wave of pleasure, her arms flailing in the air for an anchor in the storm.

Lucas continued to pump into her, his body dripping with sweat. As his weight pressed down on her, she heard him pant in her ear, "Do you love me, too, Tara?"

She reached for him, one hand in his hair, the other around his neck, and met his thrusts with her own, lifting her hips as high as they would go, taking him deeper and deeper into her body until she heard him growl his release, a white-hot explosion that dripped down her thighs, a whisper in her ear saying this was better than any dream, better than anything.

And as they lay there, tangled together in the aftermath of their passion, she brought her mouth to his. As they kissed each other, Lucas' fingers fiddling with the fabric of his old jacket, Tara could still feel the lingering heat of him inside her, filling her with a strange sense of completeness.

"Everything about this… it's so much better than any dream, Lucas."

He reached up to trace her jawline, his eyes filled with such sincere tenderness that made her chest tighten. "Good. If you want the real me, I'm here for you. Always."

She wondered how long she could keep this up.

This artful, passionate deflection of hers.

She drew musical notes on his chest, taking her time to savor the texture of his skin. "Hmmm…maybe everyone is wondering what happened to us."

"Most likely they've already heard of the fireworks

coming from your room." His teasing grin caused her cheeks to burn. She gave him an earnest shove, unable to suppress her giggles as he rolled away from her.

"Come on. We should go out before they call the police in from town to investigate." He reached down to help her up, and she let him pull her to her feet. They shared one more heated kiss before she moved to the closet while he retrieved his bag from the floor.

As they dressed, he glanced over at her. "I'm glad I brought clothes in. I hope it won't be the last time."

Only half-dressed, she crossed the room in a second and was back in his arms in a heartbeat. They fumbled with each other's clothing, lowering her panties and his pants and briefs just enough to allow their bodies to join together again.

She clung to him as they moved together on the bed one more time. When they were finally spent, she reluctantly pulled away from him, knowing they had to face the world outside her bedroom door.

Before they stepped out, she turned to him, reaching for his face with a gentle hand. He paused mid-stride under her touch, turning his lips to kiss her fingertips.

"Lucas...I...I want to be with you...the real you. Always."

He answered with a smile and, for the moment, it was enough.

CHAPTER 14

THE PROMISE

Lucas

H E FELT LIKE A BOY AGAIN, FILLED WITH AN ODD KIND of dread as he drove to his parents' house.

Following Tara's abrupt exit from last night's game and his subsequent hurried departure to follow her, Lucas knew exactly what awaited him the moment he walked through those doors.

Questions.

But he was ready for anything, because he had her in his life now. He had this beautiful, passionate, maddeningly delicious woman in his arms, under his skin, in his very soul, just as she had him in hers.

This, too, made him feel like a love-struck teenaged boy.

Once he cut the engine, Lucas reached for his phone, buried deep within his sports bag on the passenger seat. It was the first time he had looked at it since yesterday afternoon, and it had been almost a full day since then. The screen lit up with a barrage of messages and a list of missed calls from Derek, his parents, and a number not on his contacts list. He sighed, locking the phone again before stepping out into the midday sun. He'd deal with it all later.

He'd barely taken a few steps towards the house before the phone vibrated. The screen showed Derek Torreblanca as the caller's name, which he quickly swiped to accept.

"Delgado, you're alive!" Derek's voice boomed through the phone. "How are you, man? I thought you were dead or something. I almost—almost—called Benny because you didn't take my calls yesterday."

Lucas chuckled at the mention of their team manager. "Well, I'm glad you didn't. The poor man would have over-reacted and filed a Missing Persons report. I had a game with the village kids yesterday evening…and, then, spent the rest of it with a very special lady."

"What? Fuck me, you did?" The excitement in Derek's voice carried clearly through the line.

"You were right, you know. I found love here in the country, just like you said."

"Seriously? Who is she? Do I know her?" The questions came in rapid fire. "Do I get to be the best man?"

"Easy, easy." He tried to laugh it off, but the source of his hesitation was very clear: a shared vulnerability after a night of secrets and revelations. He didn't want to be presumptuous or betray Tara's trust by revealing too much too soon. "I don't want to jinx it, but I've met the girl of my dreams."

"Wow, that's amazing. And, yeah, you sound like someone in love."

Did he really? It felt like it, his body still humming with the desire to see Tara again—hold her, touch her, *be* with her.

"I don't know about that," he replied lightly.

"I can't wait to hear more when things work out, man," Derek said. "After all this time, you deserve to be happy. I'm glad you met your mystery lady."

"Thanks, Derek. You'll be the first to know."

"Great!" There was a hesitant pause, before his friend continued in a more serious tone. "We'll still see each other at the training camp in a few weeks, won't we? You're not just gonna ride off into the sunset, are you?"

"No, I won't leave you or the team in a lurch, I promise." Lucas spied a figure peering through the curtains of the bungalow. "Enjoy the rest of your vacation, Derek. Give my regards to your family."

"Will do. Take care, brother."

"Take care, man. See you in Manila."

As soon as the call disconnected, his mother appeared in the doorway, her eyes studying him intently, while his father followed behind her with a concerned expression.

"Lucas, is everything okay?" Mercy's voice was laced with worry. "How's Tara?"

"We've been trying to reach you since last night," Luis interjected. "Has Marife brought her guitar back?"

He took a deep breath and put on what he hoped was a reassuring smile. "Everything's fine, Ma. I found her last night on the road leading to the farm and took her back to the villa. I didn't leave until I was sure she was alright. She got the guitar this morning and was tuning it when I left."

His father shook his head, guilt evident on his face. "We shouldn't have asked her to perform. I feel responsible for what happened to that poor girl."

"Hey," Lucas said gently, placing a hand on his father's shoulder. "It wasn't anyone's fault but my own, Pa. I shouldn't have displayed my feelings like a lovesick teenager."

His mother moved closer to console him, wrapping him in a warm embrace. "Oh, Lucas, you can't blame yourself for wanting to show the world how you feel for Tara. I saw it on your face the moment I mentioned her name when you first got here. It was as clear as day."

"I'm glad you looked after her, as a real man should," said his father, gesturing for them to take seats in the living room. "How is she holding up?"

"She slept," he answered simply as he settled on the couch, the aches and pain of his body back in full force after the stress and emotional rollercoaster of the previous night. "She ate something this morning, too. The women at the farm will take good care of her."

"Maybe we should call her parents," Mercy suggested. "They live in Iloilo, don't they?"

Lucas shook his head. "No, Tara doesn't want her family to worry. She made me promise not to make a big deal of it. But I'll make sure she's okay, Ma. I'll keep checking on her."

"We'll make sure to look after Tara, too," added Luis. "If she still wants to see us."

"Of course she does, Pa. She felt guilty for walking out—she felt as if she let all of you down. She kept apologizing the whole time."

"It's all that fame…all that pressure on such a sensitive young woman," Mercy said, her voice cracking, tears brimming at the corners of her eyes. "Her being alone in that farm—it isn't natural. She should be out in the world enjoying her life. She should be with people who love her."

"You can start with me, Ma." Closing his eyes, Lucas leaned back and allowed himself to be vulnerable in front of his parents. "I've loved Tara for the longest time, ever since we first met in college. She's the reason I've never really had serious relationships…I helped her get home one time, during a storm. After that, I followed her around like a fool, but never talked to her again. Yeah, it's really stupid, but she's always had me."

A heavy silence settled over the room. He'd expected disbelief, perhaps uncertainty, maybe even mild judgment. When he opened his eyes, he saw only concern on the faces of his parents.

"Our hearts choose who to love without asking for permission," his mother finally said, reaching over to pat his hand. "Yours did, Lucas, and it chose very well."

"We're happy you found Tara again, after all these years," said his father, a small smile on his usually somber face. "Must be fate. It took some time, but you're with her now, aren't you?"

Lucas took a deep breath as he looked at both his parents in turn, not knowing how to react to such a sincere show of support. Perhaps they really did see the depth of his feelings, the road he'd taken just to reach this point in his life.

With a gentle smile, Mercy got to her feet. "Have you had lunch?

He shook his head. "I had some coffee and eggs at the farm earlier, but it's been a long night."

"Your mother has put aside some food for you," Luis said, nodding towards the kitchen. "Maybe you can bring some for Tara, too, if you want to check on her later."

"Thank you, Pa." He stood up and excused himself quietly, retreating to the guestroom.

Once inside, Lucas sat down on the edge of the bed, his mind swirling with thoughts of Tara. His phone vibrated again, startling him out of his trance. It was that number— the one not listed in his contacts. Curiosity piqued, he picked up the call.

"Lucas Delgado."

"Hello, this is Jasmine Samontes," said the caller briskly. It was a woman's voice, crisp and no-nonsense. "I'm the manager of Tara Galvez."

Surprised, he stared at the screen for a few seconds before replying, wondering how in the world could Tara's manager have any business with him. "How can I help you?"

"Help me?" she scoffed. "You have some explaining to do, Delgado. How dare you pull a stunt like that with Tara!"

He bristled at her tone but forced himself to remain calm. "I'm not sure what you're talking about, Ms. Samontes."

"Last night's game?" Jasmine snapped. "My source told me all about it—how Tara ran off upset after you tried to pull some romantic publicity stunt. Are you in some kind of relationship with her? Have you been hiding it from the public? For how long?"

Taken aback by her questioning, Lucas hesitated before responding. "This is a private matter between Tara and me."

"Private?" Jasmine's voice rose in disbelief. "You made it my business when she ran off in the middle of a song she's performed a million times. You have no idea how sensitive Tara is. You can't even begin to fathom what she's got at stake right now."

Lucas clenched his jaw, frustrated by her accusations but keenly aware of the truth in her words.

"I will never hurt her," he said firmly, clutching the phone so tightly in his hand he thought it might snap in half.

"Maybe you don't think you will, but if you keep putting her in situations that threaten her well-being, you'll have to answer to me. There's so much pressure on her for her tenth-anniversary album, Delgado. If you fuck things up for her, there will be hell to pay." He could hear her breathing down the line, clearly worked up and ready for battle.

Lucas took a deep breath. "I'll make sure she's not hurt or overwhelmed. I will protect her. I promise you that."

"Good," Jasmine retorted. "But just so we're clear, I don't know you. I trust you even less."

"Then know this, Ms. Samontes. I love Tara Galvez. I believe in her talent, and I believe in her."

Jasmine's silence hung heavy on the line for a moment before she spoke again. "You better not screw this up or I will destroy you, personally *and* professionally. She's my best friend, and if you really love her, make sure she doesn't spiral into self-doubt and never come back."

"Understood," Lucas replied curtly, feeling the leaden weight of his own promise.

"Goodbye, Delgado."

"Goodbye, Ms. Samontes."

As he ended the call, he stared out the window, heart pounding as the gravity of the situation began to sink in. He laid back on the pillows and closed his eyes, focusing on the image of Tara kissing him, telling him her songs had always been meant for him.

Lucas awoke with a start; the room was already filled with dusky shadows. Disoriented, he glanced at his phone next to him, noting the time—almost six in the evening. A message from his father informed him that both parents were away for their Monday night meeting with the town's co-operative heads. Hunger gnawed at him, and he realized he hadn't eaten all day.

Alone in the darkened house, his thoughts circled back to Tara, not realizing he was already dialing her number.

She picked up after three rings. "Hello, how was your day?"

"Truthfully?" A lump formed in his throat as he thought of her in the big villa on her own. His mother was right; this wonderful, beautiful woman deserved to be with people who loved her. "It hasn't been complete without you."

She laughed. "We only saw each other this morning."

"Well, I can't see you enough. Can I come over for dinner?"

"Yes," came her immediate response. "I'll see you soon."

After hanging up, he quickly took a shower and changed into fresh clothes. Soon, he was on the road to Galvez Farms. Once he reached the gates, he made use of Fred's remote control.

As he drove through the entrance, a night watchman greeted him with a respectful nod, showing no hint of surprise at his access privileges. "Good evening, Sir Lucas."

As he navigated the dirt road leading to the villa, he spotted Tara waiting for him on the front porch, silhouetted in the waning sunlight.

He knew then he would never let her go or hurt her.

This was love. It didn't matter if it was old or new, fated or just coincidence. What mattered was the woman who stood at the end of the road.

As soon as the car rolled to a stop, he sprang out the door, bolting up the steps two at a time. As soon as he reached her side, she leaped into his arms, her laughter like the sweetest music.

He had that love now, and he was determined to keep it.

Believe me
When I say goodbye
In a halting whisper
Believe me
When I turn away
From the promise in your eyes

Believe me
That I'm never sorry
For loving you
Believe me
That I walk away
Before I no longer could

~ Excerpt from 'Believe Me'
Lyrics and music by Tara Galvez
I Remember You, Esta Melodia Records

CHAPTER 15

THE ETERNITY

Tara

T WAS NEARLY DINNER TIME, REMINISCENT OF THEIR reunion earlier that month. She stood on the porch, her gaze fixed on the cloud of dust billowing behind the approaching car.

She began to wonder if this was nothing more than a beautiful dream, remnants of an old love only she could remember, a mirage born from the longing in her heart.

But no, it was all real.

The sound of Lucas' voice on the phone, asking if he could come over, was real. His touch from their night together, still lingering on her skin, was real. The taste and scent of him, all over her, musky and irresistible, was real.

And maybe, just maybe, he really did love her.

As the SUV came to a halt before the house, Tara's pulse quickened. She watched as he emerged from the vehicle, heartbreakingly handsome as always with a big grin on his face. A stream of giggles escaped her as she crossed the last few inches that separated them and sprang into his arms. He caught her effortlessly, kissing her as if they hadn't seen each other for an eternity.

Perhaps it felt that way. Perhaps love had a way of changing everything—the perception of time, memories, and the weight of waiting.

The world around them seemed to blur into nothingness as they stumbled through the threshold, still locked in their passionate embrace.

"Are we alone?" Lucas gasped as he came up for air. His eyes focused on her face before he breathed out, "And how is it that you get more and more beautiful every time I see you?"

"Y-yes," Tara stammered, her cheeks flushing. "I told the women I'd be fine for the evening."

He chuckled in satisfaction, his hands beginning to roam down her body as she turned to lock the door behind them. "I'm starving for dinner, but I'm even hungrier for you."

"Me, too," she said softly, leaning against the wood once the final bolt was in place.

"Good." He pressed his body to hers, hand reaching under the hem of her sundress. His fingers traveled slowly up her thigh, tracing the curve of her hip and waist, before finally settling on a lace-covered breast. "Let's take this slowly, love. Slower than last night."

"I'd like that," she whispered. "I'd like that very much."

So unlike last night's frenzied passion, they undressed each other slowly. He lowered the straps of her dress first, kissing the bare skin underneath; her bra and panties followed, her most intimate places worshipped by his lips and tongue. She did the same, with his shirt, pants and underwear; her hands traced every inch of muscle and bronzed skin, their path followed by her mouth. There was no urgency; instead, there was an almost reverent sense of intimacy.

He guided her to the middle of the carpet and kissed her hand before he laid down on his back, wondrously naked, his cock jutting out proudly. He held out his arms to her, with the simplest yet most erotic command, "Ride me."

She straddled his lap and began to move her hips, grinding against him without penetration, arching her back as pleasure coursed through her veins. Lucas cupped her breasts, kneading the soft flesh, flicking the nipples with gentle fingers, creating a delicious friction that left her soaked and aching for more.

As if sensing her need, he positioned himself at her entrance, his hands firmly gripping her hips. Slowly, deliberately, he entered her, filling her completely, causing her breath to catch in her throat.

"I'm all yours, love. I've only ever been yours."

Something about the way he said the words—with such tender surrender—that made the dam of her feelings break.

Tara rode him, slowly at first, then faster and faster, her body creating a harmony of pleasure that soon reached fever pitch. Lucas followed her lead, pumping into her with a fervor that spoke of a love long denied, his hands gripping her hips like a lifeline.

And the tears came, streaming down her face as she called out his name. Love, ecstasy, pain…she wasn't sure anymore, trembling on the precipice of her most intense climax yet. She wasn't even sure who came first, only that it was a deep, grunting thrust from him that pushed her over the edge.

Heart racing, she collapsed on top of him, the scent of his sweat and the lingering musk of their lovemaking filling her nostrils. A few rogue tears slipped from her eyes, splashing onto his chest.

"Hey," he murmured, his fingers brushing the damp hair from her forehead. "It's okay. I love you." He guided her up to a seated position, cradling her in his arms as she pressed feather-light kisses to his heated skin.

"I missed you," she muttered into his bicep.

"God, I missed you too."

The sincerity of his tone made her chest ache, but she chose to focus on the ridiculous sweetness of their exchange. "We sound like lovesick teenagers."

"Maybe we still are, making up for lost time."

She buried her face in his shoulder, taking deep breaths

against his skin, trying to stem the tide of emotions bubbling up within her.

"I don't want to lose any more time with you, Tara," Lucas went on. "I'll be here for as long as you want me, for as much as you need me. You set the pace—you command, and I'll follow."

His words almost triggered a fresh wave of tears, but she bit her lip to keep them at bay. "Why are you so wonderful?"

"Because I don't want to screw this up," he replied gently. "I don't want to lose you again."

Talking about her feelings had always been something she shied away from, but with him, she found the courage to slowly bare her heart. It was terrifying, but it was a start.

"We never really lost each other," she began. "Just like you, I haven't had what you could call a relationship. I've met men, sure, mostly while touring abroad. But… I'd pull away, knowing I couldn't offer them anything real."

"Tell me, love," he encouraged, stroking her bare back as he kissed the crown of her head.

"About six years ago, there was Andrew, hands down the most serious of them all. I met him in San Francisco during the kick-off concert of my North America tour. He followed me for three weeks, but I ended it in D.C., right before flying to Vancouver. It didn't feel right, stringing someone along, knowing I could never give them what they wanted."

"That's pretty fair," he murmured. "It sounds like the right thing to do."

She nodded and tilted her head up to meet his gaze. "Do you know what I did after breaking up with him?"

"What did you do?" His curiosity was tinged with warmth.

"I watched your game on my phone. You made two incredible three-pointers in the last few minutes, making your team back then win by a point. Until now, I believe that was the game that convinced your team now to take you in a trade." She smiled sadly at the memory; she'd regretted hurting Andrew more than she'd actually felt the loss of her short-term lover. Watching Lucas play had been the best thing to do to console herself.

"I'm glad you got traded. I never did like your old team. Their franchise player was—and still is—an ass. The refs should call him more often for travelling—he can't even dribble to save his life." She blushed, looking away when she saw his eyes widen at her comments. "I've hated men I didn't even know just because they fouled you or blocked your shot." Laughter escaped her then, and she gave in to it with as much of her heart as she could.

Lucas joined in, his chuckle rich and infectious. "You've been stalking me, woman. That's very bad."

"Yeah. Not as bad as you, but equally guilty."

He brought his head down to kiss her lips, tightening his arms around her. She could still hear and feel the laughter rumbling in his chest. "Seems like we've always been connected, in one way or another, haven't we?"

She nodded. "I guess, but I still don't understand *this*… We'll never get the time that we lost back, Lucas."

He sighed. "It hurts like hell to think about it, but maybe that isn't how love is supposed to be."

"What do you mean?"

"I don't think we're meant to understand it, or question how it works," he said patiently. "We're supposed to live it, you know?"

She smiled, smoothing down thick locks of his wavy hair that stood up all over his head. "You should be the one writing love songs."

He grinned in response. "Well, I'm available for bookings, but for you I'm always free. Just say the word."

"Can you help me understand that kind of love, then? Teach me about the kind of love that we actually get to live?"

"I would do anything for you, Tara. Anything you want."

"Show me," she said, almost shyly. "Show me right here, now, on the floor."

He didn't need any further prompting; he guided her down onto the pile of their discarded clothes and made her lie down. His eyes darkened with desire as he explored her body with gentle touches. His palm and fingers worked expertly to make her wet, just as she saw that he was more than ready, too.

Lucas shifted to his knees, spreading her legs wide while he positioned himself between her thighs. Carefully, he lifted her hips and entered her. The sensation was overwhelming, filling her completely.

"Let me know how you want it." His pace was slow and steady, yet beautifully unyielding. His grip on her ankles was firm and controlling, yet somehow comforting in its dominance.

"Harder," she commanded, and he complied, driving into her with passionate vigor that made her moan in delight. "Faster," she urged, and he increased his pace, their bodies moving together rhythmically.

"Your hand," she gasped, and without hesitation, he placed one hand on her clit as he continued to slam into her.

Their crescendo built, her breasts bouncing and her arms reaching wildly in the air; she couldn't care less at her wanton state as she found herself on the brink of ecstasy. "Yes, Lucas, yes!"

She hit the peak with an explosion, her body trembling as she moaned his name again and again. The sound seemingly made his control slip away, and he was on top of her, fingers threaded through hers in an almost painful grip, pounding into her with such force that left her breathless and spinning towards a second orgasm.

Lucas came hard with her this time, his body stiffening, eyes closed as he shook uncontrollably and collapsed on top of her.

"You're a great teacher," Tara murmured, wrapping her arms around him.

He took her compliment with a gasping laugh and a groggy response. "Happy to teach you more, after dinner and all night long."

They took their time to get up from the floor and share the night's meal before retreating to her bedroom, where they made love again and again until dawn.

In the weeks that followed, they took their time to live in love.

The days were filled with simple pleasures: running around the farm and tending to her garden in the early morning, sharing breakfasts of *pan de sal* and fresh coffee, and sneaking into her room at midday to make slow, sensuous love.

Afternoons were spent with her music and his art, Tara sitting at the front porch strumming her guitar and singing as she weaved new melodies from their own unfolding love story; Lucas lounging from across her, always sketching with a smile on his face.

Evenings were for exploring the local villages in search of fresh fruits and street food, having dinner in the villa or in any of the tiny eateries they found along their drives, and making love in every corner of the house once they were alone.

It was everything she'd ever wanted—the only man she had ever truly loved, in the only place that had ever truly felt like home.

But no matter how hard she wished she could hold on to this time forever, she knew it wasn't possible.

The real world awaited them both.

CHAPTER 16

THE GOODBYE

Lucas

I T WAS HIS LAST DAY IN THE VILLAGE.

Lucas tried not to think so much of the minutes ticking away as drove towards the main villa of Galvez Farms. The sunrise was beautiful, after all, and at the end of the road, he was going to see Tara again. He was determined to savor every precious moment he had left with her.

His heart fell when he saw the empty front porch. Over the past few weeks, she'd always been there waiting for him, a smile of her face.

As he pulled into his usual spot, Fred appeared with a wide grin. "Sir Lucas, thank you again for getting me the new motorbike. It's been really helpful in getting around the village more quickly. Not to mention Dodie picked a beauty."

Lucas had to smile at the foreman's enthusiasm. "It's very well deserved by you and your family, Fred. Least I could do for you and your wife looking out for Tara."

"Well, I just wanted to wish you good luck in the Philippine Cup. We're all rooting for a third championship. I may or may not have bet half a year's wages on you getting the Finals MVP, too."

Lucas chuckled at the statement. "In that case, I'll do my best not to let you down, or Marife will have my head."

"She'll hang me upside down on a tree covered by red ants, more like, but it's gonna be worth it." The older man rubbed the back of his neck before he continued. "By the way, Sir Lucas, do you need anything for Manila? Anything we can do for you before you go?"

Lucas shook his head. "I'm fine, but thanks for asking. I'll be driving back to the airport and return my car there."

"Miss Tara asked my wife to help prepare the *biko* for you to bring back to Manila. I told Fe she'd better make it extra special, you know, for good luck."

Emotion caught in Lucas' throat at the mention of Tara's thoughtfulness. Over these weeks, he'd grown to love her *biko*, which she'd prepared for him every Saturday. "Thank you. Please tell Marife I appreciate it."

Fred nodded. "Will do, Sir Lucas."

"Can you do me a favor, Fred, and keep an eye on Tara? If she needs anything…just let my parents know."

"There's no need to worry, Sir Lucas," the foreman said with a confident, reassuring smile. "Miss Tara is loved and protected in this village."

"That's very good to hear." Lucas extended a hand. "I'll see you all again soon."

"All the best, Sir Lucas." Fred shook his hand briskly. "Oh, if you're looking for Miss Tara, she's in her garden. She's been there for a while now."

"Thanks, Fred."

With a murmured farewell and a tip of his hat, the foreman was gone.

As Lucas made his way down the familiar path, the breeze made Tara's flowers dance gracefully in the sunlight. He could still remember her standing in their midst all those weeks ago, moments before their first kiss.

His beautiful, sensitive angel, welcomed by his parents into their lives with open arms. Every Sunday, they would attend Mass at the village chapel, followed by a generous lunch his mother had lovingly prepared. On their last Sunday together, Tara had sung for his parents, her delicate voice accompanied by the strumming of an old guitar that belonged to his father. In that moment, he'd realized just how perfectly Tara fit into his family—a gentle soul who thrived under the tender care and love that surrounded her.

Upon reaching the end of the path, Lucas stood at the edge of Tara's garden, watching her for a few moments as she moved among her white and gold flowers. She seemed to sense his presence, pausing for a moment before turning to smile at him over her shoulder. He approached her slowly and, as he reached her side, wrapped his arms around her from behind. He pressed gentle kisses to her cheeks and hair, breathing in her scent.

"Hi." Tara turned in his embrace and angled her face up to his, eyes fluttering close.

He brought his lips down to hers, in a kiss that felt like a wondrous eternity wrapped in a few fleeting breaths.

Everything he had ever wanted, now in his arms. The constant aches he felt from his injuries were nothing—nothing—compared to the searing emptiness brought about by their impending separation.

"Uh, I've got the bread," he mumbled, clinging to the reality of their breakfast routine in hopes of not losing himself to the pain. "Left it in the car. I got worried when you weren't on the porch."

She gave him an apologetic smile as she shook her head. "It's okay. Sorry, I lost track of time. I wanted to get some flowers for you."

"Why?"

"Because I felt like it." With a heavy sigh, she stepped out of his arms, her gaze drifting to an overflowing basket of blossoms on the ground.

"Something wrong?" He reached her hand before she could move further away. "Are you okay?"

"Of course not. How could I be, when you're leaving to-morrow? No more Saturday *biko*, Lucas, no more Sundays…"

Her voice caught as she averted her eyes, her shoulders shaking.

In a desperate, helpless bid to comfort her, he fumbled for words. "I'll come back—weekends, whenever I can. We can see each other in Manila, right? I'll get you flights and courtside tickets to all my games… You could even stay with me in my apartment if you like, or I could stay with you, or I could book you into a hotel…"

"Sounds like you've got it all figured out," she said quietly, slipping out of his grasp.

"What do you want me to say, Tara?" He could only stare at her back uncertainly, heart pounding. He wanted nothing more than to grab her and ride off into the sunset, never to be seen again, just like Derek had said.

He watched as she deftly plucked a white chrysanthemum from its stem, weighing it in her hand.

"I don't know," she finally said, her voice barely audible above the gentle rustle of leaves. "Just tell me, Lucas, what do you really want?"

He blinked at the question, taken aback by its simplicity. It sounded so obvious, but as he searched for an answer, he realized just how little he understood what it truly meant.

"I don't understand, love," he admitted.

She walked up to him, her eyes glistening with unshed tears as she put the white flower in his shirt pocket. Her hand lingered over his heart, then reached up to caress his cheek.

"What do you really want?" she repeated, her voice stronger this time.

"I want you," he replied, choosing the clearest, truest answer he had. "I've always wanted you. I want a life with you in it."

Her gaze held his. "I've always wanted you, too. A life with you in it. But I don't know what kind of life that would be. I still don't."

He felt a strange sense of relief wash over him. "Neither do I, but maybe we can find out together."

"Together…" she echoed, the word almost disappearing into the wind. "You make it sound so easy."

With that, she let go of him, moving out of his reach and into the middle of her garden, ensconced in the safety of her flowering plants. Between them stood pots upon pots of roses. It looked like Tara was protecting herself with their thorns.

"I don't know what else to say, Tara."

She sighed as she delicately ran her hands over clusters of white blooms. "Do you remember what I told you the night of the game?"

"Tara, I—"

"I've been running from my own head. I've been hiding out here, hoping I don't fall apart long enough to make music that still means something. To make sure I still mean something. You made me believe I meant something, and I'll never forget that."

"But you know what I really want?" she sobbed, wiping at her eyes almost angrily. "I want a life where you're happy and healthy and loved. I want a life where I can give you all of myself without getting scared."

"Scared of what?" His throat tightened, feeling the pain of the vulnerability she had somehow trusted him to know.

"Of everything, Lucas. Of falling apart again and again, thinking I'll never be good enough. Of you getting hurt again and again, right in front of me. I'm in fucking pieces, and I'm scared you're going to get torn apart any day, too. We found each other after all these years, and for what?"

"For *us*," he answered hoarsely. "For us to be together. For you to be loved by me."

"What about you—your heart, your art, your body? Don't you care about what happens to you? Because…I do. I care."

In that moment, realization struck him like lightning—she loved him. She had never said it, but he knew it as surely as he knew his own name. He closed the distance between them and reached for her hand, pulling her gently out of the cluster of plants.

"I love you, Tara. Please, tell me you love me too."

"Will you stay with me if I do?" she countered softly. "I'm far from perfect, but I'll take good care of you."

He smiled at her, as bravely as he could. "You've always been perfect to me. Always. But staying here…it's not that simple."

"I never thought it was," she murmured, smiling back with sad eyes. "I thought I'd try anyway. Someone taught me to take chances even when we're scared shitless. He taught me about real love that way."

He understood the weight of their choices—the life they could have together, and the life that pulled him away. Not knowing what else to do, he embraced her. "Sounds like a very wise man."

She didn't resist, hugging him right back. "Yeah. I'm going to miss him when he's not around here anymore."

He kissed the top of her head. "He's going to miss you, too."

Tara laid her head against his chest, ear to his heart, not saying anything for a while. After some time, she pulled away just enough to look up at him. "Will you stay the day?"

He nodded, not trusting himself to speak with the growing lump in his throat. He stepped around her to retrieve her basket from the ground and held it out to her. His actions reminded him of the first time he'd seen her in the garden. The first time they kissed.

"Shall I get started on the coffee?" Tara took the basket and tilted her head in the direction of the villa.

"Please. I'll get the bread."

After retrieving their *pan de sal* from the car, he went into the kitchen to see her preparing their breakfast as she did every morning these past weeks. Standing on the balcony, he watched her move gracefully about, her hair swinging like a silk waterfall as she worked, her hands performing each task with her customary elegance.

This could be last time they shared their quiet, unhurried

rituals, so he tried to memorize every detail of her: the way her shirt clung to her slender frame, the gentle curve of her wrists as she poured water, the delicate sweep of her eyelashes as she blinked.

When she finally set down their tray of coffee and bread before him, he reached across the table and took her hand.

"I love you," he said simply.

She smiled in response. "Eat up. Good thing the *pan de sal* hasn't gone cold yet."

He didn't let her hand go, even as she tried to wriggle it out of his grip. "Tara, will you…would you like to join my family for dinner this evening? My mother's cooking my *despedida* meal, and my uncle and his wife are joining us, too."

She lowered her head, gaze fixated on the wooden surface between them. "I d-don't think it's a very good idea. For me to come over a-and all, especially tonight."

The stammer and sadness in her voice were enough to break his heart. "Why?"

"You know why." She managed to pull her hand out of his, using it to rub at the corner of her eye. She was crying quietly.

"Tara, please…"

She averted her eyes towards the field of coconut trees. "This isn't easy, Lucas. I don't want your parents to worry about me. You know how they are. I don't want to ruin your last day with them."

"I'm sure you won't," he insisted, pleadingly, almost desperately.

"Won't cause a scene like the first time I was there?"

"It's not your fault."

"Of course it's my fault." She shook her head vehemently, tears sliding down her cheeks. She shakily tried to wipe them away, but not too successfully. "The game, too, that was my fault. I care too much and I end up losing too much. I know that very well and I know exactly what's gonna happen."

He could only stare at her, at a loss for words. She was everything he had ever wanted. Now, he was the source of her pain.

"Please don't make this any harder than it already is," she sobbed. "Please, Lucas. Just do me this favor."

He stood up, made his way to her side, and knelt next to her so they were eye to eye. "Kiss me, then. Let's forget everything. Let's forget that it hurts. Just for now."

Eyes wide, she hesitated for only a second before she threw herself into his arms.

Their lips met hungrily, breakfast and the world around them forgotten.

He carried her up to her bedroom, where they undressed each other. He reveled in the feeling of her soft skin beneath his fingertips, etching every curve and contour into his mind. He tasted every inch of her body, lapping up the sheer sweetness of her like a dying man.

He took her on the middle of the floor, pumping into her as she cried his name out and gasped for more, rubbing her clit and her nipples in turn until they were pebble-hard from the pleasure of his touch. She straddled him on her bed, riding him slowly, drawing out every sensation as he thrust upward to meet her; soon urgency took over, and they both gave in to moans that shook the villa. He took her from behind as she leaned over her windowsill, bare breasts bobbing wantonly in the air, the gauzy white curtains wrapped around their heated bodies.

As they showered together before lunch, it was her turn to kneel before him in the bathroom, on the tiles that had witnessed so many passionate encounters. She gave his cock all the attention he so craved, rolling it between her breasts before putting the length of him into her mouth; as she massaged and tugged at his balls, his release exploded in her lips, punctuated by his own strangled shouts.

After lunch, she packed up the special *biko* for his trip, in a beautiful box woven from palm leaves, decorating the packaging with flowers from her own garden. His heart twisted painfully as she gave him tips on how to keep the rice cake fresh the moment he reached his Manila apartment.

That afternoon, they didn't bother to retreat to the porch. Instead, she led him back up to her room, where they made love again and again, clinging to each other as their borrowed time came to a hazy, heady standstill, measured only in caresses, kisses, embraces, and promises of a love that would endure.

It was nearly sunset when they collapsed on the middle of the bed, arms and legs entwined, shaky and sweaty and breathless, but never quite sated. Eventually, as the shadows grew longer and the minutes shorter, they rose to dress, languidly, prolonging the inevitable farewell with sto-len kisses. Half-dressed, he took her one last time against the walls of her bedroom, her legs wrapped around him. When they reached the peak together, night was upon them.

They finished dressing, then made their way down to the living room, where the box of *biko* awaited on the coffee table, sealed and ready for the journey ahead. Tara picked it up with a smile and carefully placed the parcel in his hands.

"It will last you a while…I made it extra special, too, with lots of coconut flakes and calamansi syrup."

"Thank you." It was all he could utter, after all was said and done in their love story.

Tara linked her arm through his as they made their way out to the porch and down the steps. "Don't ask me again, Lucas."

"I won't."

She nodded, seemingly appeased, as she watched him put the box onto the passenger seat of the SUV. When he closed the door, the sound rang out with poignant finality.

He took a deep breath as he turned to face her. "I guess that's it."

It was goodbye.

"Yes, I guess." She smiled as she reached out to caress his cheek. "Knock 'em dead, Number One, okay?"

He returned her smile, nodding at her request. "Do you think…it would be okay if I saw you tomorrow morning be-fore I go? So you can kiss me good luck?"

She laughed, the sound mournful and broken, and shook her head. "Oh, Lucas."

"No?"

She held out her arms and he went into them. Without another word, their lips met, tenderly, each tracing the other. He pressed his mouth and nose to her forehead, closing his eyes as he took in her scent. He could drown in it and die happy.

"No," she whispered into his neck. "I want to remember us as we are now. So, good luck, Lucas."

"I love you," he replied, the words catching on the night breeze. "I'll call you…every time I can. I promise. Will you let me know once you're back in Manila, too?"

She looked up at him and nodded. With one last look into her eyes, he, finally, painfully, reluctantly, let her go.

Without another word, Lucas climbed into the car, knowing that he was leaving behind a part of himself. He drove away; before making the turn towards the farm gates, he stopped the vehicle and stepped out, unable to resist looking at her one last time before the sight of her was swallowed by the fading light.

Tara stood at her usual spot on the front porch, waving him off. She blew him a kiss, and he caught it, holding it close to his heart, even as the winding road took him farther and farther away from the woman he loved.

I still look at the screen
Hoping it would be your message
Hoping somehow you found me

I still look at the screen
Hoping your picture would be there
Happy, smiling, truly alive

With tears in my eyes
In the quiet hours of dawn
Though I know
You will never be there

I still look at the screen

~ Excerpt from 'Screen'
Lyrics and music by Tara Galvez
I Remember You, Esta Melodia Records

CHAPTER 17

THE DIAMOND

Tara

T HE NOTES FROM HER GUITAR HUNG IN THE WARM AIR as she strummed and hummed, piecing together fragments of a new song.

Tara sat on the front porch of the villa, savoring the gentler touch of the late afternoon sun. Gone were the days of soft breezes; the encroaching heat of the summer months reminded her of how quickly time had changed everything.

Glancing at her phone on the porch table, silent and unmoving, she felt a familiar wave of guilt. Lucas had tried calling her often, but she had refused to take his calls. He'd sent messages too: telling her he'd made it back to Manila, thanking her for the *biko*, updating her about their training camp and the start of the Philippine Cup Conference. But eventually, his messages dwindled to short weekly texts and then nothing at all.

A small part of her was relieved that he had decided not to keep messaging her. It was an odd emptiness akin to what she'd felt before he came into her life, and in some ways, it was a comfort. No melody or words could fill the void, no adoration from fans could replace it. Since then, she'd stopped going out of the farm, immersing herself in her music instead.

Despite occasional invitations from Mercy Delgado, who sent formal messages through well-meaning villagers bearing notes to her at the farm gates, she remained secluded. Mercy had asked how she was and if she'd want to visit their home, anytime Tara was free.

Tara had once penned a response back, delivered by Marife and Fred along with a crate of Galvez Farms' new line of flavored *nata de coco*. She had thanked Lucas' mother for her kindness, but Tara's songs had a deadline. It had hurt to push away the family who had shown her nothing but love.

Love.

It was the strangest emotion, imbued with as much power to destroy as to shape the world around her. Love had made her music come to life; it had also shattered her heart into a million pieces. At the end of it all, she was still alone.

"Excuse me, Miss Tara?" a gentle voice called out.

She looked up to see Marife ascending the porch steps with another woman in tow—Lucas' mother. A strange sense of *déjà vu* washed over Tara as she recalled the first time she saw Lucas that year, standing on these very steps. Her heart clenched at the memory.

Quickly setting her guitar aside, Tara stood up, feeling a pang of guilt at the concern etched on Mercy's face. Instead of the anger or frustration she had expected, she was met with only a mother's worry. As Marife murmured an apology for disturbing her, she could only nod in response, unable to find her voice.

"Would you like something to drink, Mrs. Delgado?" the housekeeper asked politely.

"Thank you, but I'm fine," Mercy replied. "Good afternoon, Tara."

"Good afternoon, Mrs. Delgado." The formal address left her before she could stop herself. "Would you like to sit down?"

With a quiet nod, Marife retreated, leaving the two women alone on the porch.

Mercy nodded her thanks and took a seat on one of the rattan sofas. Her tone was gentle yet probing when she spoke. "Tell me, Tara, how are you? We've all been so worried about you, especially Lucas."

At the mention of his name, tears welled up in her eyes. On her own, she could pretend—but with the very reality of Lucas' mother sitting in front of her, the pain of loss hit her almost like a physical blow.

"I'm so sorry, Mercy." She sank into a chair, her voice

cracking as she tried to hold back her emotions. "I'm so sorry for not accepting your invitations."

The older woman shook her head, her eyes searching Tara's face. "It's entirely your choice whether or not you want to visit us, dear, but you shouldn't let it bother you. Luis and I are more concerned on how you're holding up…being here on your own, running the business, making your music. It's a lot to take on."

Unable to bear the concerned scrutiny from Lucas' mother, Tara closed her eyes, feeling hot tears brimming over once more. "These past few months have been so hard, trying to convince myself that I don't need anyone. I thought I could just carry on with the life that I've been used to for so many years. But the truth is, nothing's been the same."

"Since Lucas left?" Mercy asked gently.

Tara took a deep breath, allowing tears to escape to relieve the pressure inside. "I miss him. I miss being part of your family. I just couldn't be part of a life where he keeps getting hurt and broken…I wanted to take care of him, to make sure he is happy and healthy, but now he's so far away…" Her voice trailed off as she realized that even Lucas' parents didn't know the full picture of his health.

Mercy took a seat beside her, putting a comforting hand on her shoulder. "Is that why you've pushed us away? You're afraid of what being part of his life—of loving him—might cost you?"

Tara nodded, her chest heaving with sobs.

"He's been fighting through all that damage to his knee

and his back like a true warrior," Mercy said, sighing softly. "It's hard seeing Lucas put on that brave face all the time, of course. It never gets easier, even after a few years."

Tara stared at her. "How did you know?"

"Lucas is my son, Tara. I know when he's hurting, when he's sad, when he's happy. I started seeing the signs a while back, whenever we visited him in Manila or when he'd visit us at our house in the city."

Mercy paused, her gaze steady. "I never asked him about his injuries, allowing him space to admit the truth when he was ready. Lucas is a smart man, Tara. He knows exactly what he's doing, and when he's ready, he will tell us the truth."

She reached out and took Tara's hand, giving it a comforting squeeze. "I'm glad Lucas has told you about his injuries, but I am even happier that he found you. He really does love you, Tara. I've never seen him so happy, so fulfilled, when you were together."

Tara could only shake her head in disbelief. "I'm sorry."

"For what?" Mercy tilted her head, studying Tara's face. "Sorry that you loved my son too? Sorry that you came into our lives and made us feel what it's like to have another daughter, one as talented and beautiful as you?"

"I just…I couldn't be someone who could keep loving Lucas even if I see him slowly being broken on the court. I feel so helpless about that. I just wanted to be there for him, but not in the way he wants…"

"Lucas loves you for being yourself, Tara," Mercy told her patiently. "He loved you even when you were just a face on a music video and a voice in a song. He has done nothing but adore you all these years; I've seen his collection of your records in his apartment, heard him play your songs on his phone when he thought no one could hear."

"Mercy, I love him, too…loved him since I was a girl. He's only ever been the one for me."

The older woman nodded, her eyes and smile filled with understanding. "You have no idea how much and how deeply Lucas loves you. Maybe you should give him a chance to love you as best as he could. It might surprise you."

Through her tears, Tara felt a small smile tug at the corner of her own lips as a memory surfaced. "Lucas told me the night of the basketball game that he felt whole again when he was with me."

"Yes, he does feel like that," Mercy confirmed, her own smile getting bigger. "It was written all over his face, the first time I told him you were at the village."

Tara breathed out slowly and squeezed Mercy's hand. "I just want you and Luis to know…I had the best time of my life with your family. I've never felt so welcomed and loved. I'll always be grateful. And I hope…you're not disappointed in me."

"No, never." Mercy reached out and smoothed her hair. "We're very proud of you, Tara. Whatever happens, you'll always be welcome in our lives."

"I appreciate that." Wiping away at the remnants of her tears with the back of her hand, Tara gave the older woman a grateful smile. "I'll be leaving the village soon, maybe in a few weeks, so I'm glad I got to see you. I was just putting the finishing touches on the last song for my third album."

"Ah, I see. And where will you be going, back to Manila?"

Tara nodded. "I'll need to arrange the songs with producers and then hit the studio. After that, I might take a page out of Lucas' book and stay with my parents in Iloilo. Once the album is out, I'll be busy for a few months with promotions…and then, that's it for me, I guess."

"Will you be coming back here or…?" Mercy's voice trailed off as she regarded Tara curiously.

"I don't know yet. My recording contract will be over by then, so it would be nice to have some real time to myself for a while. Perhaps we'll see each other when you pass by Iloilo."

Mercy nodded and leaned in to kiss Tara on the cheeks and forehead, before giving her a big hug. "Perhaps we can spend a Sunday together. Luis and I would love to hear you sing for us again. We missed you."

Tara returned the embrace tightly. "I missed you both, too."

As she pulled away, the older woman reached into her bag on the coffee table and produced a colorful envelope that appeared to be meticulously hand-painted. Upon closer inspection, it was made of dried coconut skin, with a discreet logo on the corner bearing the name 'Delgado Homemade Products.'

"Lucas was going to give this to you," said Mercy as she got to her feet, carefully placing the envelope on the table.

"He'd hoped you would join us for his *despedida* the night before he left."

"He did ask me, but I didn't think it was a good idea at the time." Tara felt a lump in her throat as she recalled how many times she'd refused him. "I suppose it's too late for regrets now."

Mercy picked up her bag and made her way to the steps. Before descending, she turned to Tara and gave her hand a squeeze. "It's never too late."

She shook her head. "I'm just glad he and his team are doing so well at the tournament. That's enough for me."

Mercy gave her a long look before she spoke. "Someday soon, we'll all break and get hurt, and we'll be able to piece ourselves back together when there's someone holding us up, someone holding us together. That's love, Tara. Don't deny yourself of that love."

"Maybe someday," she replied simply, giving the older woman a reassuring smile.

After they exchanged goodbyes, Tara watched Mercy walk down the steps, heading in the direction of the farm gates. As the distance between them grew, she once more felt a sense of desolation that had become all too familiar to her in recent months.

She turned her attention to the envelope Lucas' mother had given her. She carefully opened it and pulled out a folded piece of paper. Her breath hitched as something small and shiny rolled gracefully out, landing on the wood with a soft clink.

A ring.

It was a golden ring adorned with a delicate diamond, the gem shaped like a basketball.

Surprised, Tara unfolded the paper to reveal a familiar scene in pencil and pastel: herself standing amidst a garden of white and golden flowers, bathed in the soft glow of morning sunlight. But this time, Lucas was there too, drawn kneeling before her just as he had done at the basketball court. The difference was that in this picture, he held out the very same ring that now lay before her. At the bottom right corner, the drawing was signed and dated—the last day they had spent together.

Tears welled up in her eyes as the realization hit her like a tidal wave. Lucas had wanted her to join him and his family for dinner that same night. He'd asked repeatedly, insisted and pleaded upon it.

He had intended to propose.

And, yet, she had never given him the chance—never gave herself a chance to make her songs, her dreams, finally a reality.

She remembered her own words to him, said in the very same garden. Real love was about taking chances even in the face of fear.

Love, she thought dazedly.

One word, an emotion; it had haunted and taunted her for years. She'd desperately tried to capture it in her lyrics, through her stories told in song. It had never been enough, because she'd never lived it.

Now, she finally had it. All she had to do was be brave enough to walk into its unknown embrace.

"Lucas," she whispered, the name disappearing into the wind, melting in the heat of a summer she'd thought would only be filled with memories and lonely nights.

She fell to her knees on the porch, her heart threatening to burst from her chest. Through the torrent of tears blurring her vision, Tara Galvez finally saw the truth—a love for Lucas Delgado that could not be denied any longer.

CHAPTER 18

THE GIFT

Lucas

THROUGH THE FLOOR-TO-CEILING WINDOWS OF HIS high-rise apartment, he stood and watched the city below come to life as night approached. Lucas knew he should have been exhausted after a long day of practice and strategizing with his team, but instead, he was wide awake, consumed by a gnawing emptiness.

Stand and watch. That was what he did.

Two days ago, he stood and watched as his shots met only the board and then nothing, the ball bouncing to the hardwood floor in defeat as he missed two free throws in the final minute of Game Six. He stood and watched as the opposing team won the game by one point, forcing the Philippine Cup Finals series into a sudden-death Game Seven.

It was *déjà vu*, too. They were playing against the same team they faced in last year's Finals, where the double-overtime seventh game had been nothing short of brutal, leaving physical and emotional scars.

"Fuck this," Lucas muttered under his breath, rubbing at his sore ribs. One well-placed elbow and he was done for.

The silence of the apartment was broken only by the rhythmic ticking of the wall clock. Sighing, he glanced over to check the time, taking in the carefully curated display of team photos and framed victory jerseys on his living room walls. Each and every one of them spoke of his success as an athlete.

He had paid enough for it—with time, discipline, pain, loneliness, and pretension. He had played the game in and out of the court, now here he stood, watching the world go by, wanting—needing—only one thing.

Her presence in his life.

All he could do was remember what he had lost, what he now desperately missed.

The warmth of her mouth on his, their kisses shared during meals and drives. Their lovemaking, passionate and tender, in the hidden corners of her villa, her skin flushed and glowing under the moonlight. Her sweet vanilla smell seem to have followed him, too, wrapping him in a gentle embrace he longed for. The way she would say his name became the melody that haunted his dreams.

Lucas closed his eyes and let himself be carried away by the vision of her stirring *biko*, focused and content; he could see her snipping at the flowers in her garden, sunlight filtering through her long dark hair, turning it into a halo of soft light.

His hands itched to draw her again, to bring her back to life on paper, but he knew that he couldn't. Not after leaving the last drawing—the one meant to accompany his proposal—along with the ring at his parents' house. It was a cowardly act, but he was better off without those reminders of what could have been.

As he watched the sunset cover the city in orange hues and dark shadows, memory of that day more than three months ago came flooding back. The day he'd returned to his apartment and unpacked the box of *biko* Tara had sent with him. He recalled the large plastic container nestled in a woven basket, adorned with flowers from her garden.

But there was another gift hidden among the petals—a silver compact disc with only his name written on it in black marker.

He'd eaten his way through the *biko*, all on his own, in three days' time. He never had the heart or the courage, however, to listen to the CD. He'd stashed it away instead, in a final act of self-preservation.

He hesitated for a moment before making his way into the bedroom. He located the CD inside the top drawer of his night table, now part of his collection of Tara's albums. His heart pounded as he inserted the disc into the home theatre system, unsure of what was in it but knowing that hearing her voice, beautifully immortal in recording, would be the only way to keep her close.

There was a soft whirring sound for the first thirty seconds, then her voice came through, tentative and sweet.

"Hi, Lucas." There was a pause as he heard her take a deep breath. *"I don't really know what to say. That's pretty strange, isn't it? After all, I rely on my talent to mince words and stuff like that."*

There was another pause. Tara laughed softly. *"What am I doing, anyway?"*

A short silence followed, then guitar chords began to fill the air.

"I call this song 'Untold.' I started writing it a couple of nights ago, when I couldn't stop thinking about you and…you know, being with you. I had the best time ever these past weeks, Lucas. I'll never forget how kind you've been to me. Thanks for everything."

She breathed deeply once more. *"Well, here goes nothing. Hope you like it."*

Tara began to sing.

You said that you were sorry
That you don't need me no more
You said that you were leaving
And walked right out the door

Baby, how many times have you hurt me?
I truly have stopped counting
How many times have you left me?
Standing alone while it was raining

You said that all was wrong
That nothing works when we're together
You said we would only be lying
If we keep talking of forever

So go on, tell me
Whatever you want to say
Go on, be true
There seems to be no other way

Tell me I'm not the ideal
I know all your reasons why
Tell me I'll never be strong
That I'm always lacking in your eyes

Tell me everything that hurts
This forever hopeful heart of mine
Tell me how to make you stay
But, baby, just don't tell me goodbye

Her voice broke at the end of the song. The closing chords melded to the subdued whirring of the CD, then there was nothing.

Nothing, except for a lone tear escaping his eye, burning its way down his cheek.

Nothing, except for his emotions that he hadn't allowed to surface in far too long, and his love, now gone unanswered by a phone number that would not pick up, a message recipient that would never respond.

He sat on the floor in front of the speakers, unaware of how much time had passed since the CD stopped playing. He stared at the city lights reflected on his walls, lost in the regret of not staying when she'd asked him to.

I'm far from perfect, but I'll take good care of you. It had been her greatest declaration of love. Now he was left with nothing.

Suddenly, the doorbell rang, breaking through the stillness of his darkened apartment. Startled, he realized he rarely had visitors, especially at this hour. He considered the possibilities as he rose to his feet and fumbled for a lamp switch nearby; perhaps it was the team trainer or even their manager checking up on him. But when he opened the door, his heart skipped a beat when he saw neither of them.

Instead, he saw Tara.

He blinked hard, trying to determine if he was dreaming or hallucinating from the pain in his body—or perhaps even his heart.

But she spoke, her voice unmistakable, "Hi, Lucas. I'm sorry for bothering you. I know it's late—"

She couldn't finish her sentence before he wrapped his arms around her, as if holding her tightly enough would ensure she wouldn't vanish into thin air. To his relief, she didn't disappear; she was solid and real in his embrace.

"Lucas," Tara whispered, her breath warm against his chest, "I missed you. I really missed you. I'm sorry if I hurt you."

He couldn't find the words to respond, still in shock at her sudden appearance. Instead, he buried his nose in her hair, inhaling her familiar vanilla scent, reveling in the warmth and feel of her body pressed against his.

Without another word, he guided her into the apartment, locking the door behind them. In a heartbeat, their lips met in a passionate reunion, her hands tangling in his hair. As they kissed, he heard something fall to the floor with a dull thud but paid no attention to it, utterly consumed by her touch.

"Love," he finally managed to say between kisses, "I missed you, too." He then proceeded to shower her cheeks, nose, and chin with tender pecks, eliciting giggles and strangled sobs.

Tara clung to him, her slender arms wrapped securely around his neck. He welcomed her weight, but reality loomed over him like a dark cloud.

Hesitantly, he released her, steadying her on her feet. "Are you real?"

She nodded, smiling slightly. "Look, Lucas, I'm so sorry for this...I just wanted to—"

"Stop apologizing, love, please." Taking her hand, he led

her to the couch and motioned for her to sit down. "Would you like something to drink?"

"Water, please," she said, wiping her cheeks with the back of her hand.

He hesitated for a second, reluctant to let go of her even for a moment. But he hurried to the fridge to retrieve a bottle of water, returning as quickly as possible to sit beside her.

"So…how are you?" As he handed over the water, he spied her backpack that had fallen on the carpet earlier. He'd been too preoccupied to pay attention to anything but her presence in his apartment.

"I've been traveling since early morning. I left the farm after midnight." She took a long sip of the water before continuing. "I came straight here to see you."

"Why?" His one question was a mixture of shock, happiness, and disbelief. "Why didn't you call me at least? I could have picked you up from the airport or asked someone to drive you over."

Tara offered him a sad smile as she look him straight in the eye. "I wasn't even sure if you wanted to see me or talk to me after everything that happened. But I know how it feels when everything's hanging in the balance, when your next move could either make you win or lose it all—everything you've worked hard and sacrificed for."

Just like in her recording, she took a deep breath and went on, the emotion in her voice going straight to his heart. "I came to tell you that whatever it is you feel now, and whatever happens tomorrow, you won't be in it alone."

He inched closer and took her hand, relieved when she didn't pull it away. "How did you find me?"

He wasn't sure if she giggled or snorted—perhaps both. "Jasmine knew where you lived. She knew about what happened between us at the farm. She made me promise I'd let her know whether or not this would work out, that is, my 'crazy romance heroine stunt.'" She made quote marks with her fingers as she mentioned the phrase.

"This is a stunt?"

"I told her I wanted to see you after the game two days ago," Tara explained. "She tried to talk me out of it. We ended up with a compromise. If you break my heart, I would let her 'destroy him professionally and personally.'" She rolled her eyes as she said the last few words.

Lucas chuckled. "Not the first time I heard those. She warned back then there would be hell to pay if I hurt you."

"Yeah, she told me she called you the day after we… um…" She blushed and looked away. "Anyway, she knew what was going on the whole time."

He nodded solemnly. "Very scary lady."

They smiled at each other, before he decided to take her in his arms again. She went into them with a contented sigh.

"Lucas…I'm not sure if your mother told you…" As she spoke, her fingers danced over his heart just as she rested her body trustingly against his.

"Told me about what, love?"

"About my decision to…slow down."

He smiled down at her. "She did mention a few weeks

ago you told her you've decided not to renew your recording contract."

Tara nodded, explaining that she'd finished writing her songs. Lucas listened as she went on about the work needed for her album and what would follow its release—media appearances, press conferences, promotional shows. She had turned down the offer of a grand concert tour throughout the country and worldwide.

"I'll still be writing music once this is over," she declared, a note of excitement in her voice. "But on my own terms, maybe as an indie."

"Won't there be at least one concert for your tenth anniversary?" he teased. "One I could see from the front row?"

"For three nights, around this time next year. We've decided to name it after my third album, *Our Love Replay.*"

"Our love," he echoed. "Replay."

She pulled away to look up at him. "Lucas—"

"I love it," he murmured.

She smiled at the compliment. "I knew you would."

Nothing more was said as he leaned in to capture her mouth. They kissed deeply, hungrily, until the room was covered in the sultry embrace of night. As they broke away for air, he carefully guided her down onto the carpet, his hands deftly unbuttoning her blouse and jeans before helping her out of her panties. He quickly undressed, his desire almost at breaking point at the sight of her beautiful and vulnerable beneath him.

He lowered his lips to hers, exploring the curves of her

body he so desperately missed. His mouth found her nipples, teasing them until she let out breathy gasps of pleasure. Moving lower, he trailed kisses along her stomach, his tongue dipping into her navel before continuing its journey downward. Spreading her legs, he licked and nipped at the delicate flesh between her thighs, until she was writhing with the need for release. With his lips, tongue, and fingers, he brought her to the peak.

"Lucas," Tara gasped, her body trembling with the force of her climax, "I love you."

Still reeling from the force her confession, he covered her body with his and entered her in one powerful thrust.

"Did you just…?" When she nodded, whispering those three precious words once more, he lost himself in her completely.

"Say it again," he urged as he moved within her, thrusting faster and deeper as his hands cupped her breasts. "Tell me again."

"I love you," she cried out as she clung to him, meeting his hips with hers. "I have always loved you."

As Tara's moans grew louder, reaching a crescendo that echoed throughout the building, he joined her in a release that left them both breathless and shaking.

The night was a symphony of love, their bodies intertwining on his bed again and again, in the middle of which they shared a late dinner of *siopao* and vegetable *chop suey* on his dining table, the end of their meal marked with her riding him on the wooden surface, taking him to new heights.

As morning light filtered through the curtains, he stirred, his arms still wrapped around her. He took in the sight of her peaceful face, her lashes resting gently on her cheeks, her breath a soft whisper against his chest.

She was real—and she loved him.

In that moment, he felt invincible.

Slowly, carefully, he eased her from his embrace, tucking the blankets around her. He longed to wake her, to share his own decision with her—the one that would shape both of their futures, regardless of the outcome of tonight's game.

Instead, Lucas sent a message to his team manager, informing him that he was on his way to their meeting and asking for one last favor. He wasn't sure whether or not Tara would like to be at the game, but the choice was ultimately hers to make—just as she'd chosen to love him.

He scribbled a note and left it with his extra key next to her phone on the bedside table. With one last lingering look at her, he kissed her on the forehead. "See you after the game. I love you."

As he locked the door behind him and stepped out into the world, he knew he was finally ready to take one last shot.

I want to go home
To the days of years past
When the breeze was soft
Laughter was easy
Love was a possibility

I want to go home
To the days that never were
When I saw you
Found you
Loved you

I want to go home
To the days when you were there
When I had your voice
Your light
Your heartbeat

I want to go home

~ Excerpt from 'Home'
Lyrics and music by Tara Galvez
I Remember You, Esta Melodia Records

CHAPTER 19

THE VICTORY

Tara

HER HEART RACED AS THE BLACK VOLVO CAME TO A stop outside the sports arena. The noise of the crowd inside was already reverberating through the air around them.

Tara glanced at Simon, the assistant manager of Lucas' team who had accompanied her on the trip. The car itself had been sent by the team's owner, for her exclusive use before and after the game.

"Here we are, Miss Galvez." Simon opened the car door and stepped out into the crisp air, holding out a hand to assist her. He had a quiet, confident demeanor that calmed her.

As she took his hand and stepped out, she noticed that it wasn't the main entrance she'd seen countless times on television. This entryway was more discreet, shrouded in shadows.

"VIP access only," Simon explained, catching her curious gaze. "Reserved for league and team officials, and the occasional high-profile personality." He smiled at her knowingly. "Of course, you're a VIP too, Miss Galvez. Everybody knows you. My wife loves your songs."

"Thank you," she murmured. It felt strange to be considered important when all she wanted to do was to support the man she loved.

Following Simon down a dimly-lit corridor, Tara felt the air grow heavy with tension. She slowed her steps as they approached a small door, which seemed to be positioned directly under the bleachers.

"Straight to courtside," Simon declared, almost proudly.

"Could you give me a minute?" She gripped his arm just as he reached for the knob. She needed a moment to collect herself before facing the public eye once more.

"Of course," he replied, stepping forward to peek through the tiny door left ajar. "The teams are already on the floor warming up."

The thought of seeing Lucas play up close was enough to propel her forward. Determinedly, she took Simon's arm and walked out with him.

Stepping into the dazzling lights of the arena, Tara was momentarily blinded by their intensity. The noise from the warmup and enthusiastic crowd washed over her. The audience waved red and white balloons, streamers, and flags, creating a sea of vibrant colors. Among the banners, she spotted many with Lucas' face on them.

"Right this way, Miss Galvez," Simon said, patiently guiding her to her seat. As she glanced around, searching for any glimpse of Lucas among the players on the court, a familiar warmth enveloped her.

"My dear, surprise!" Mercy Delgado pulled her into quick hug.

"It's so nice to see you here, Tara," said Luis as he appeared at his wife's shoulder and embraced her, before gesturing to three adjacent seats meters away from the bench of Lucas' team.

"Thank you, Simon," Tara said, her earlier anxiety ebbing away at the presence of Lucas' parents.

"Anytime, Miss Galvez," Simon replied with a smile, before joining the bench of his team.

Mercy took Tara's hand and gestured for her to sit down. "How have you been, dear?"

Tara smiled. "I'm fine, thank you. I came to Manila to support Lucas." Her heart swelled with pride as she admitted this truth aloud.

"Ah, we are so proud of you and happy with your decision," Mercy beamed, her eyes shining with approval.

Her gaze wandered back to the court, trying to catch a glimpse of Lucas in action. Just then, a sudden hush fell over the arena, followed by an excited chatter that spread like wildfire. A courtside reporter had spotted Tara and called out her name, sending ripples of excitement through the audience. "Tara Galvez is here!"

"Look, dear." Mercy gave her a gentle nudge and pointed to the giant screens hanging above the court. Tara's face appeared on them, causing people to cheer and whoop with delight. Heat rose to her cheeks, but at the encouragement of Lucas' parents, she mustered the courage to stand up and wave, acknowledging the crowd.

As she did so, her eyes finally found Lucas standing at the free throw line, his attention drawn by the noise. Their gazes met across the distance, and she felt her heart skip a beat when he gave her a smile and a wink. He dribbled the ball towards the baseline close to where she stood, and mouthed, *"For you,"* before turning and making a flawless three-point jump shot, making the crowd roar in approval. She applauded along with the rest of the arena before resuming her seat.

The noise in the building grew thunderous as the game commenced. Her eyes remained fixed on Lucas, watching as he expertly maneuvered through the sea of opposing players, his every move an intricate dance of agility and skill. As she watched him glide across the court, just as she had all those years ago from under the acacia tree, she felt the weight of her past doubts lifting, replaced by a newfound sense of freedom.

It wasn't lost on her how the opposing team used ruthless tactics to stop Lucas—double and even triple teams, deliberate fouls from players off the bench, and an in-your-face defense from his shooting guard counterpart. Midway through the game, there was a charging foul that could have very well broken Lucas' ribs. By the time the last two minutes rolled about, Tara's breath had nearly left her body, more so when the scores tied.

"Come on, Lucas!" she cheered, her voice joining the chorus of thousands.

Lucas' team had possession of the ball thirty seconds before the final buzzer. A teammate tossed him the ball from the inbound line. The seconds ticked by as the shot clock started running down. Twelve to shoot. Eight. Someone stepped in front of him; he evaded easily. Six. Two players tried to block his way. Four seconds.

She watched with bated breath as Lucas lined up for a pivotal three-pointer. His hands came up, lightning-quick. The ball soared through the air, arcing gracefully before hitting the board, then spun around the hoop. Pandemonium erupted when the ball swished through the net.

"Delgado. Three points!"

As Lucas raced past her, his eyes met hers for a brief moment, and he blew her a kiss. The crowd's attention shifted momentarily to Tara, their eyes wide and curious, before snapping back to the action unfolding on the court.

The other team had six seconds to shoot. The ball moved quickly, almost desperately, towards the outside line, for an attempt to tie the score. It never had a chance, with Lucas in its way. The guard made the shot, clean and well-aimed, but Lucas leaped into the air and blocked the ball, sending it out of bounds.

The buzzer rang out like a triumphant anthem, signaling the end of the game and the three-peat of Lucas' team as the Philippine Cup champions. Red and white confetti and balloons cascaded down like a euphoric rainfall as the arena filled with the raucous sounds of victory.

She jumped to her feet with the rest of the crowd, clapping and cheering at the top of her lungs. Lucas' teammates hoisted him onto their shoulders, and their coach joined him in a jubilant ride around the court. Next to her, she watched Lucas' parents embrace each other tightly, tears streaming down his mother's face.

As the celebration continued on the court, league officials presented trophies to both teams, with short speeches honoring their efforts throughout the season. And then came the moment: Lucas was awarded the Philippine Cup Finals Most Valuable Player for the third year in a row.

The Commissioner of the league held up a hand for silence, a diplomatic smile on his wizened face. "Our three-time Philippine Cup Finals MVP, Lucas Delgado, will be making a statement. To our ladies and gentlemen of the press, we would be happy to answer all your questions at our post-game press conference later tonight."

Still cradling his MVP trophy in one arm, Lucas shook the Commissioner's hand and took the microphone the other man held out, ready to address the crowd.

"Thank you, everyone!" Lucas began, with his familiar infectious grin. "I am truly humbled by your support and love throughout this incredible journey. First of all, I must thank my incredible teammates, our owner, and coaching staff for their tireless effort and dedication in leading us to our third conference championship in a row."

"I want to congratulate you for giving us a fantastic Philippine Cup Finals series," he added with a smile, bowing his head respectfully towards the opposing team's player and coach. "You guys pushed us to be better, and for that, we are grateful."

Lucas paused for a few seconds, his gaze taking in the sea of faces before him. "I'm sure everyone has heard one or two rumors about how I would end the Philippine Cup, aside from partying with my team." The statement was met with appreciative laughter and whistles from all over the arena.

"Ladies and gentlemen, please allow me to put these rumors to rest. I will not be joining the Arabian Falcons in Abu Dhabi as their coach, or in any other capacity. I had a generous offer from Sheikh Khalfan, which I had to regretfully turn down. My heart is in the Philippines and in this league."

Tara could hear excited murmurs rising from the crowd.

"There is no trade in my future, not in the next tournament or the following season. I won't be a free agent, either, and I won't be coaching in any league or college in the foreseeable future. My contract is with my team, and that is where it will end."

A hush of disbelief descended on the crowd, followed by a roar of questions that people were asking each other. The media and sportscasters surrounding Lucas kicked up into a frenzy, pressing around him on the court.

He took the reaction in stride, gracefully acknowledging them with a patient smile. "I am ending the Philippine Cup with my retirement from basketball. Tonight was my last game. Being a part of this championship legacy has been the greatest honor of my career. I would like to thank the millions of fans all over the world, especially the ones present in this arena tonight. None of this would have been possible without you."

Lucas looked up to the bleachers; on the giant screens, Tara could see the sincere gratitude in his eyes. "I will still be the league's biggest fan, but I would no longer be playing or working in it. It's time for me to become a spectator and cheer on my teammates, especially the tireless Derek Torreblanca, from the sidelines." He grinned as fans whistled at the mention of his teammate's name.

"But rest assured, I will always love the game that gave a young boy from Iloilo more than he ever dared to dream." He held up his MVP trophy in the air. "Once again, thank you very much, from the bottom of my heart."

The arena exploded with sound again as more balloons and confetti rained down, accompanied by the unfurling of a giant banner bearing Lucas' jersey number one. The court announcer's voice boomed through the speakers, declaring that the team was retiring his number in honor of all that he had achieved. "Please join us in giving a farewell ovation to our three-time Philippine Cup Finals MVP, Lucas Delgado!"

Tara rose to her feet, clapping and cheering until her hands stung and her voice grew hoarse, as the true meaning of Lucas' decision settled on the fringes of her overwhelmed mind. It was a slow, dawning realization that warmed her heart.

He had made his choice.

Through the throng of photographers and reports rushing to surround Lucas, his eyes searched the crowd and met hers.

"I love you," he mouthed.

For the first time in her life, Tara felt truly unafraid, truly free, as she gave him her answer.

"I love you, too."

CHAPTER 20

THE BEGINNING

Lucas

THE DASHBOARD CLOCK READ 1:58 AM AS DEREK'S car rolled to a stop outside his apartment building. From the passenger seat, Lucas gave his friend a tired, contented grin.

"I thought that press conference would never end," he said, shaking his head. "I almost fell asleep in my bird's nest soup."

"Yeah," Derek concurred. "They should have served the meal before the questions."

"I second that." Lucas reached for his bag in the backseat and gave his friend a grateful clap on the shoulder.

"Thanks for the ride, man. Officially my last one as your teammate."

"Anytime, although not the last as my friend," Derek replied, grinning. "You bastard, I can't believe you finally did it, though. And without telling me.

He swallowed hard against the knot in his throat, unable to suppress his guilt for keeping such a secret. "My body's just… it's not holding up anymore. Tried to keep moving through it for a while, but in the end, I had to make a decision."

Derek's smile faded as he took in Lucas' somber expression. "That bad, huh? I mean, I've seen the wraps they made you wear sometimes, but, damn. Never thought it was that serious."

"Kneecaps and ribs are shot," Lucas admitted quietly. "My back muscles feel like they're barely stitched together. The double and triple teams this conference didn't help, either."

"Jesus, Lucas…" Derek sighed, his eyes reflecting a depth of understanding only a teammate could possess. "Must have been hell keeping that from us."

He nodded. "It was, but thanks for getting it, Derek. Best to quit while I'm ahead, right? Before time really catches up with me."

"Can't argue with that. We're not exactly spring chickens anymore." Derek grimaced as he ran a hand over his right knee. "This screams with every rebound, too. After I jump and then my feet hit the ground…fuck."

"Tell me about it," Lucas chuckled. "You should get that properly seen to one of these days, maybe rest it for a while before the next conference. When I spent that time at my parents' house, I barely played—just ran every day to keep the tank in shape."

Curiosity flickered across Derek's face. "So, that mystery woman you mentioned before…it was Tara Galvez, wasn't it? She had quite the effect on the crowd tonight…I knew she was gorgeous, but *man*, in person? No wonder you couldn't stay away."

"Yeah, it was her," Lucas confirmed, feeling a smile tug at his lips at the admiration in Derek's voice.

"Good for you, man," Derek said, giving him a hearty slap on the back. "No more staring at your Spotify playlist like a lovesick puppy, then?"

"Guess not." Lucas picked up his sports bag and pushed the passenger door open. "See you in a few days at the party, yeah?"

"Wouldn't miss it." Derek gave him a parting wave and thumbs-up. "Talk to you soon. Good night."

"Good night. Thanks again." Lucas shut the door and watched Derek drive off into the night. He lingered on the pavement until the red tail lights blurred into the distance.

His last ride as Torreblanca's teammate was right. They still had a team victory party next weekend, not to mention a basketball camp for kids over the summer, but tonight really did mark the end of one chapter and the beginning of another.

The phone in his pocket felt like a tiny anchor, grounding him in this moment of transition. Pulling it out, he quickly scrolled through a few new messages. One was from his older brother in Iloilo, who had to stay home with his heavily pregnant wife, their second child due any minute. His younger brother had already called earlier from Toronto, amidst cheers and shouts of congratulations from an entire community center filled with supporters. An earlier message from his father confirmed that both his parents were back at their hotel and enjoying room service.

And there it was, punctuated by an emoji with a heart on its lips, Tara's brief yet affectionate text from a few hours ago: *'home, luv u'*

Lucas ambled towards the entrance of his building, nodding to the night security guard stationed at the lobby, who promptly beamed and called out merrily, "Congratulations, Sir Lucas!"

After thanking the guard and wishing him a good morning ahead, he took the elevator to the top floor and quickly made his way to his apartment. He fumbled for his keys at the entrance, but before he could find the right one, the door swung open.

Tara stood at the threshold, wearing his bathrobe. She was a vision of casual intimacy, her unbound hair contrasting sharply with the white terrycloth.

"Congratulations, Number One," she breathed, stepping into his space, her arms winding around him.

"Thanks," he managed, voice rough with surprise at

seeing her awake and awaiting his arrival. He pulled her closer and crushed his mouth to hers, for a taste of his real victory. She moaned in satisfaction, reaching up to wrap her arms around his neck as she deepened the kiss, using her tongue to trace the inside of his mouth.

Breathless, he broke away only long enough to secure their privacy. His bag dropped forgotten to the floor as he drew her back into his arms, but something glinted sharply on the coffee table, demanding his attention.

Her diamond.

"What…how did you get this?" Lucas crossed the living room for a closer look, heart thundering in his ears.

It took only a few strides and one trembling touch to confirm it was the very same ring. He quickly lifted his fingers away from the coldness of the gold band, sinking onto the couch as apprehension washed over him.

Tara's touch was cool on his burning cheek as she took a seat beside him. "Your mother brought it to me, along with your drawing."

He shook his head, surprise, disbelief, and nerves churning in his stomach. "I didn't want to be presumptuous, or to pressure you…"

"You were very persistent in getting me to that *despedida*, to be fair," she commented gently, leaning her head against his shoulder. "But I suppose I had more stubborn in me that day compared to you. The heart tends to have the instinct for protecting itself when badly hurt."

"Was it because I didn't stay when you asked me to?"

He lifted her chin to look into those heart-stopping eyes. One look all those years ago was all it took—and he'd been hers ever since.

She nodded, blinking hard and fast as her gaze reluctantly met his.

He leaned in and pressed his lips to hers before saying, "I'm so sorry.

She cupped his face in her hands. "I forgive you, but that doesn't mean you're not a big, bumbling idiot, because you still are."

"I hope that's not because I decided to retire without telling you. I wanted to tell you last night, and this morning, but…everything just happened so quickly." The words spilled out, honest and vulnerable. "Since I left the village all those months ago, I couldn't stop thinking about what kind of life I really wanted to have. Basketball has given me so much, but not without a price…was I willing to keep paying it, with every single fucking bone in my body?"

"Oh, Lucas." She reached up to tenderly cup his cheek. "It's your life, your choice. I'm here to love you right through it. Even if you decided not to retire, I'll be right here, too."

"No," he countered fiercely, "it's not just my life anymore. It's ours, together. I want a life with you in it. A life where I don't keep hurting you or myself all the damn time."

Hope painted her features with a luminous glow. "It sounds like a great life, Lucas."

"More than you know, love. I've invested in my parents' businesses as an equal partner and even now we're looking to expand, to grow with the community, especially in cottage industries. I've put capital into Antique's local cooperatives, too, to help the people who had looked after your family and mine."

She nodded, her eyes lighting up. "Yes, that would make a lot of people very happy."

"I'm glad you agree." He nuzzled her nose with his. "I love you."

"Love you too."

He reached for the ring and looked closely at her face, trying to gauge her reaction. "Tell me, love, would you like to have this?"

Tara looked thoughtful for a moment before responding, "I don't know, was this meant for me? Because the man on the drawing clearly knew what he was doing. I'm not getting the same vibe right now."

Lucas lowered himself to the floor on one knee, not bothering to disguise his wince as he felt something crack in protest. Heart pounding, he held the ring out to her. "Is this better?"

Tara stood up before him, a playful grin spreading across her face as she took the diamond and held it up to the light. "Well, to be honest, I want you. But if it's part of the deal, why not? If I get to have you stay with me forever."

He wasted no time in pulling her into his arms, joy quickly replacing his earlier doubts as they collapsed onto the couch. "Is that a yes?"

She nodded. "Always yes, remember? Since our first night together, I have always said yes."

"God, yes, you did." He pulled away to gently take the ring from her grip and slide it onto her waiting finger. Overwhelmed, he kissed her passionately, lingeringly. "I love you."

"Alright," she said, in a soft yet businesslike voice. "I accept. Let's seal the deal, love."

Before he could fully comprehend her words, she climbed onto his lap with a graceful fluidity that took him back to their first time together in the SUV outside her villa. Her hands deftly unbuttoned his shirt while he fumbled with the belt of her robe, revealing her naked body underneath as he pushed the soft terrycloth off her shoulders.

"Always prepared for you," she murmured, as she offered up her breasts to his hungry gaze.

His hands hovered above her, itching to touch, but before his fingers could reach her flushed skin, she had already slid down to her knees on the floor. She skillfully removed his shoes, pants, and briefs, and managed to tug off his polo shirt with his assistance. She parted his legs and took him into her hands, not needing much effort to bring him to full arousal.

"God, Tara," he groaned as her hands wrapped around him, stroking the length, kneading the balls. She traced the contours of his thighs and pelvis with the tip of her tongue, every flick sending his hips bucking off the couch.

"More, love… please," Lucas gasped, the plea torn from the very edges of his reason, as she sucked and pumped him into her mouth.

And she gave—more pace, more pressure, more depth. She didn't just seal a deal—she claimed her rightful possession of him and his heart.

"Ah, fuck…" Lucas cried out as his climax shattered through him with a force that shook the entire building. He didn't care if his voice carried beyond the walls of the apartment; let the world know he belonged to Tara Galvez now.

When he came back down, spiraling from the heights of ecstasy, he found her gazing up at him, her chest adorned with the evidence of his release.

"Looks like I'm yours now," she declared, her voice a velvety, teasing caress. "Completely."

"Fuck, Tara, what are you doing to me?" With a growl, he reached for her, guiding her onto her back upon the coffee table.

He knelt between her legs and brought her ring finger to his lips, sucking and tasting the salt of her skin mingled with the metallic tang of the gold band—it was an odd yet intoxicating cocktail. His other hand reached for her pussy; he groaned as he watched her hips arch hungrily towards his touch. He drew steady circles with his palm, drawing slick, sweet wetness.

Using both hands to spread her legs wider, his mouth descended on her heat, his tongue tracing the lines of desire that his touch had just charted. His tongue lapped up the taste of her, making her writhe above him, his name on her lips.

Knowing she was close, he paused to move her to the floor next to him. Slowly, he lifted her legs and entered her, filling her in a languid, unhurried rhythm. His hands cupped her breasts, his touch gliding over the sticky sheen of his own cum.

"Lucas….Lucas…" she sang, her hands clutching at the carpet as she met his hips with hers, breasts bouncing to the beat of his thrusts. "You feel so good…"

"Look at me, Tara." He put his arms around her torso, bringing her up against his own body without missing a beat. "I want your eyes on mine."

Obediently, her lashes lifted, her arms encircling his neck as their eyes locked. The world fell away, leaving only their bodies joined in passion.

"Sing for me, love," he whispered as he thrust up into her, increasing his urgency as he crushed his mouth against hers.

"Always," she murmured against his lips, matching his rhythm stroke for stroke.

As he buried himself deep one final time, he declared, for all the world to hear, "I love you."

"I love you too," she gasped, her body shaking in the throes of passion, and then their voices rose together in ecstasy, in the sweetest symphony of their love story yet.

EPILOGUE

THE STORY

Lucas

THE STAGE LIGHTS WERE DIMMED TO NEAR DARKNESS but the studio audience was charged with an energy bordering on frenetic. The setting took him right back to the first time he'd watched Tara's concert live all those years ago, from a similar discreet seat in the back row.

Lucas watched as the crew of the noontime TV show quickly moved equipment and props around the stage during the commercial break, speaking in hushed, urgent tones. People around him whispered amongst themselves, their voices melding into a low hum of excitement.

"Oh my gosh, I can't breathe," dramatically declared a young woman a few rows in front of him. "I haven't seen Tara in forever. I'm literally dying to hear her new songs. D'you think they'll be even better than the ones from her second album?"

"You bet," a female voice answered. "I heard they're already making videos of a few singles. I can't believe she won't be touring, though. I saw her in concert last time; she was *sooooo* great. We were all crying by the time she finished singing 'Home!'"

"Did you see her at the Philippine Cup Finals last summer?" another voice chimed in. "She was cheering on Lucas Delgado. Something's definitely going on between them."

Giggles erupted from the surrounding seats, followed by murmurs of agreement. "They'd make a gorgeous couple! They should have accounts all over social media. People would follow them like crazy—I would!"

"Lucas is hot," someone else commented, this time a male voice. "It's a pity he retired too soon. Sure, Derek is cute, but he doesn't have Lucas' hair and abs. He just isn't the Daddy Lucas is."

"Wouldn't surprise me if Lucas and Tara are together," said the first girl, her voice laced with the authority of an avid fan. "He announced his retirement at the end of the conference, right? And then, a few weeks later, Tara makes this press statement that she and Esta Melodia are parting ways. What does that tell you?"

As the speculation swirled around him, Lucas smiled in the safety of the studio's shadows. They were right, after all, but it felt a little odd hearing strangers exchange theories about his new life with Tara.

"Three, two, one... And we're back!"

As the floor director's countdown ended, a spotlight illuminated stage left, where one of show's regular hosts, a statuesque actress and model, stood beaming at the camera.

"Ladies and gentlemen, I have been a fan of our next very special guest since day one. This singer-songwriter, Asia's Acoustic Angel, has been my musical idol for a decade! And now, for the very first time on Philippine TV, to perform the carrier single of her latest album, *Our Love Replay*, please welcome Tara Galvez with 'Untold!'"

The studio erupted into thunderous applause, and Lucas could feel his own anticipation mirrored by the entire audience. As the lights and cameras shifted, he saw Tara sitting serenely on a wooden stool at center stage, cradling her guitar. The live-feed screens all over the studio focused on her ethereal features; her long black hair framed her face in soft waves as her eyes regarded the audience, a gentle smile on her lips.

Tara began to strum her guitar, the poignant chords resonating throughout the studio as everyone and everything else fell silent under her thrall. Each chord weaved a story of passion and longing; each lyric told a tale filled with bittersweet moments and heartfelt confessions. As the song reached its crescendo, it seemed as though the entire audience held their breath, completely entranced at Tara's performance and collectively experiencing the raw emotions that poured from her music.

The last note of her song hung in the air like a heartbroken farewell, and for a moment, time seemed to stand still. Then, as if released from an invisible grip, the world around him came alive in a rousing standing ovation.

"Wow, Tara, that was absolutely breathtaking!" the host gushed, dabbing at her eyes. "Your voice is truly one-of-a-kind, and your poetic soul shines through in every note and word you sing. I wish I had even a fraction of your talent."

"Thank you so much," Tara replied, her cheeks flushed.

"More, more! We want more!" chanted the crowd, their voices merging into a single plea for an encore.

Lucas watched the flurry among the crew—urgent whispers into headsets, the stage manager conferring with the director and producer, and the host tapping her earpiece as she awaited instructions. It was a unique kind of chaos only Tara's performance could inspire.

As he absorbed the scene before him, an image began to form in his mind—Tara, sitting onstage, bathed in light, calmly accepting the admiration and adoration that surrounded her. Lucas had started drawing again, every day, and he never ran out of subjects. Some of his drawings had even made it to the labels of Galvez Farms and Delgado Homemade Products.

Grinning widely, the host raised her hand to silence the boisterous crowd. "Alright, alright! It seems we have a unanimous decision for an encore." She turned back to Tara, eyes dancing with excitement. "It seems they simply can't get enough of you, Tara. What do you say? Do you have another love song in store for us today?"

Tara smiled, her eyes twinkling. "I think I might just have the perfect song. It's a little something I wrote many years back when I first fell in love. That feeling has always stayed with me, so I tried to capture it in each and every song I wrote."

"A feeling?" echoed the host, leaning in with unabashed curiosity. "Do tell."

"Love and longing have always been universal emotions. They're what connect us all—our shared experiences of pain and joy, of loss and discovery." Tara's voice was soft and wistful, her gaze drifting towards the studio audience. "Isn't there always that one person, for each of us? The one whose presence transcends all songs, all stories, and all memories? No matter how much we try to capture them into words or even pictures, it's never enough."

"Wow," interjected the host, a hand over her heart, "that's so profound, so romantic. Some of us could only wish to find that kind of love." A nostalgic sigh swept through the audience, as if each person were recalling their own versions of the elusive someone Tara spoke of.

In that moment, the host's gaze fell on the ring on Tara's hand. "OMG! Tara, are you engaged? Because I'm absolutely certain that is a beautiful diamond right there."

Tara's cheeks blushed a gentle pink, but she met the host's probing stare with a coy smile and a playful wink.

"Maybe," she responded, sending a ripple of excited murmurs through the crowd.

"Alright then," the host conceded, her smile never faltering. "Let's talk about your encore song. What have you chosen to perform for us today?"

Tara's smile widened, her eyes scanning the audience until they locked onto Lucas', even through the glaring stage lights and shadowy corners where he sat. He wondered if she could really see him, but it didn't matter—he knew that her heart could now see clearly into his own.

"Today, I'll be singing the first platinum single from my debut album, *Fragments of Us*," she began, her voice tender and dreamy. "It's called 'Never with You,' and I'm dedicating it to someone very special in the audience today."

She paused, her eyes fluttering down to her guitar as she positioned her fingers on the strings. "I wrote this song for him a long time ago. Now, he's here to listen to me sing it."

As the opening chords of 'Never with You' filled the air, Lucas felt his heart swell with awe, love, and pride for the woman who had captured him so completely. How far they had come—together and apart—and how beautiful the promise of their tomorrows they now had the freedom to create.

Tara's gaze lifted once more, her smile dazzling the entire studio as she began to share their story with the world.

"This is for my fiancé, Lucas."

I love you

ABOUT THE AUTHOR

Shirley Siaton writes edgy and evocative stories and poems. Her worlds are in a deliciously dark cross-section of the romance, neo-noir, action, fantasy, new adult, and contemporary genres.

She has several books of fiction and poetry released since February 2023. Her first book is the free verse collection 'Black Cat and other poems.' She writes juvenile literature as Shirley Parabia.

She is an award-winning writer, poet, and journalist in English, Filipino and Hiligaynon, lauded by the Stevan Javellana Foundation, Philippine Information Agency, and West Visayas State University. Her essays, short stories, and poems have been published internationally in print and digital media. Her multi-lingual plays have been staged in the Philippines.

Shirley is a black belt in Shotokan Karate and an international certified fitness coach. Originally from Iloilo City, she is based in the Middle East with her husband and two daughters.

ON THE WEB

Shirley's official website:
shirleysiaton.com

Complete reading guide:
shirley.pub

Subscribe to Shirley's VIP list for free exclusive updates:
newsletter.shirleysiaton.com